ABOUT THE AUTHOR

Jennifer Manson is a writer and business woman. She lives in Christchurch, New Zealand, with her husband, two teenage children and two cats. She is the author of *The Moment of Change, Tasha Stuart interviews . . .* and *The Old Occidental Writers' Hotel* and also writes for *The Press* newspaper's *at home* supplement.

Law of Attraction

Jennifer Manson

ACKNOWLEDGEMENTS

To my writing buddy, poet Kerrin P. Sharpe;

To my readers: Tanya Tremewan and Vicki Slade;

To Martz Witty, www.martz.co.nz, generous accountant, inspiring professional speaker and angel, for being a beacon of light;

To David Killick, my brilliant and indulgent editor at *The Press*;

To Charlotte Brontë and Emily Brontë, for their dreams set in wild country;

To my daughter, Alex, my son, Jono, and my wonderful husband, Paul;

Thank you.

1

We arrived in Bruges with the first of the autumn winds. A single brown leaf blew past on the footpath as I pushed open the door of the hotel.

"Wow!" I stopped just inside the entrance to breathe in the architecture, layers of white on white, light playing on carved stone and pale plaster.

I felt Lance's bag nudge the back of my legs. "Go on, these are heavy."

"No, I want to look." A sudden gust of wind pushed my hair across my face and I took a few more steps forward.

Lance walked around me. "Where's reception?"

I heard a few words of Dutch in the distance. He disappeared up a short flight of steps in the direction of the sound. His receding footsteps echoed around the expanse of the foyer and the adjacent double height restaurant with its mezzanine colonnade.

When I got to the office Lance was leaning back against the wall watching the woman behind the desk run her finger down the page of a large book. With his light fringe falling over his face and pale jumper thrown around his shoulders he looked like a Ralph Lauren Polo advertisement.

The woman had European elegance, slim with well-tailored clothes and long, dark hair. She glanced up at Lance and I saw a look of mutual admiration pass before he slowly turned to me.

"Do you have your passport, Doll?"

I searched in my bag and handed it to the woman.

"New Zealand!" she observed. "I've always wanted to go there." She took down the details.

"We've been living in England," I said. "But we're on our way home."

"You are on the third floor. Walk through towards the garden, the lift is on the right."

Lance pressed the lift call button. My eyes rested on a classical statue set into a niche. "Can we really afford this?"

"We've been camping so long I can't look at the tent again. Besides, we deserve luxury, it suits us. A last indulgence – we'll be in Wellington in a week, and then we'll really have to start being sensible."

The lift doors opened and we stepped inside. Lance wrapped his arms around me. "Come here, Gorgeous, you know hotels always remind me of our honeymoon." He pushed a knee between my thighs.

I braced my hands against his chest, holding him away. "I saw how you looked at her."

"I look, but I don't touch. And you know no-one's as sexy as you."

I relaxed and let him kiss me. His fingers spread through my hair, raking it upwards and sending a wave of pleasure down my back.

"Besides," he added, as we stumbled out of the lift, "you shag better when you're jealous."

Damn, I know it's true. Bastard.

I washed my face, savouring the luxury of spreading out my toiletries on the wide shelf after weeks of peering into a dark spongebag looking for one thing at a time. "I think I'll have a shower."

"No, I'm bored. Let's go out."

"Let me just see the view." I went to one of the dormer windows and looked over the rooftops at the assorted church towers, small domes and spikes with lightning rods and windmills in the distance.

Lance tapped his foot rapidly. "Are you ready?"

We decided on a canal boat ride to get the shape of the city. There was a stop not far from the hotel, the walk along tidy streets, clean-lined facades of colourful buildings coming right to the edge of the footpath. Locals moved purposefully, nodding greetings as they passed; the few tourists ambled slowly.

Bright yellow café umbrellas flapped as we stepped down onto the canal path. I was wearing a summer dress and the wind blew through it. I pulled Lance's jacket out from his body to wrap around me, too.

In the boat we were sheltered between the walls of the canals. The driver told jokes in three languages. I leaned back against Lance's arm, watching the city go by, laughing at his outrageous made-up translations, immediately contradicted by the driver's words.

The boat turned, going under the bridge at the entrance to the Beguinage, occupied now by Benedictine nuns. I peered inside, intrigued.

"Shall we walk back to see it properly?" Lance asked.

"Tomorrow. I'm cold now. I want a hot bath."

Later, in bed, I lay stroking his chest. Outside, the clouds had come down and a misty rain was drifting through the streets but the room felt warm and safe.

"What do you want first, a boy or a girl? I hope I'm pregnant."

"Definitely a boy, heir to the throne."

"I don't know, though, I don't see myself as the corporate lawyer's wife, coffee mornings and dinner parties, ingratiating myself with the partners for the sake of your career while you chase secretaries in short skirts."

"What do you mean? You'll be out earning your keep. Anyway, the partners will all be chasing you – that's what I love most about being with you, they all envy me. I see them, looking at you, thinking 'Lucky bastard'."

"Why do I put up with you? All my other boyfriends treated me like a princess, built me nice pedestals."

"That's where they made their mistake. Women love bad boys, and rich bad boys . . ."

"You're not rich. You spend it all."

"But I will be."

I sighed and stretched, eyes closed. "What kind of house will we have?"

Lance pulled in his cheeks and spoke in documentary tones. "A large and original double bay villa overlooking the harbour and with a fine north-facing courtyard garden. Original mouldings and fireplaces, balustraded veranda and a six-panelled dark-blue front door. Inside the house we find the beautiful but slightly shagged-out Mrs Davis and her fine brood of blond-haired, blue-eyed future prime ministers. Mr Davis works 720 hours a week at his frightfully important but exquisitely dull job, protecting oil companies from their criminally negligent money-making activities. He does, as you suggest, chase secretaries, but only as essential relief from the otherwise deadly tedium of his day-to-day working life."

I laughed but I was only half listening.

"It will be very different from London, no more tiny bed-sit and fumes and road noise and walking with heavy shopping bags back from the Tesco."

"Yes." He nodded, eyebrows pulled into theatrically sage seriousness.

"I can't wait."

2

In the morning the weather was the same, a fine drizzle that was almost fog. I held Lance as he got out of bed. "Stay here with me. It's so cold."

"Ten miles this morning if I'm going to do the marathon in November." He pulled on a fresh T-shirt and shorts and began lacing his running shoes.

"Wait then, I wrote a note to my mother, to tell her when we are arriving. You can post it on the way."

The note was on hotel paper, and I got a hotel envelope, the address in blue in the top left corner. I wrote Mum's address, put a stamp on it, and wrote "par avion", drawing a little aeroplane. "I'm such a bad daughter, I should have written ages ago."

Lance shuffled impatiently. "Get a move on, Darling. God, get her set up on email as soon as we get back."

The door shut with a click and I shivered and turned up the radiator before creeping back into bed. I buried my face in Lance's discarded T-shirt, then held it against my chest as I read. When I glanced up through the window I couldn't see any view, only the flat grey sky.

Unease crept up gradually, first making me restless, then getting me up out of the bed, pacing the floor. Shouldn't he be back by now? What time had he left?

I dressed fast, putting on whatever came to hand, then ran out the door, down the stairs, into the foyer. But what now? I paced back and forth, my eyes on the street door. Voices came from the office but what could I ask? I looked at the statue, picked up a brochure from the stand but didn't read it. My legs were shaking and I sat down on a chair below the niche. I willed Lance to stagger through the door, sweaty, saying he had got lost in the unfamiliar streets.

Minutes passed, but instead of Lance, two policemen came in. They went into the office, more voices, then came out into the foyer again with the hotelier. She looked worried. One of the policemen had a letter in his hand. I got up, walked closer, and when I was sure the letter was my own, I reached out without thinking and took it. The policeman began to speak in Dutch but the hotel owner put out a hand and spoke herself in English.

"The officer said they found this letter in the hand of someone who had collapsed near the market square."

"My husband went running, he was going to post it."

The owner turned and spoke in Dutch to the policeman. I felt my stomach heave and covered my mouth.

The woman hesitated. "I'm very sorry, Mrs Davis. We can't be sure it is your husband, but the person who was carrying the letter is dead. If you wait while I call someone to watch the desk, I will come with you."

3

"Simon, it's Julia."

"Hey, hi, great to hear from you. How are you?"

My tears choked me. I couldn't speak.

"Julia? What's wrong."

"Lance . . . Lance is dead."

The silence seemed endless.

"What happened? Was there an accident?"

"No, he was running. They think he had a heart attack."

"Fit 26 year olds don't have heart attacks." His voice was flat.

"I don't know. That's what they said. They're doing an . . ." I couldn't say the word – autopsy – it belonged back there in the cold, dead morgue. I realised I was shaking.

"Are you okay?"

I put my hand to my cheek and smeared the tears, wetting half my face.

"Do you want me to come?"

My eyes pressed themselves closed and I nodded.

"Julia? Listen, I'll come. Tell me where you are. And I'll call Mum."

"No, I'll do it. I'll do it."

This was the call I should have made first. His mother. My hand hovered over the numbers and as it rang and rang I so wanted to disconnect. Finally Sheila picked up.

"It's Julia," I said. My voice cracked.

"Julia? Julia, where are you?" She sounded slow and slurred.

"Belgium – Bruges." What to say now?

"Julia? It's the middle of the night. Is Lance there?"

I had to force myself to say it.

"He went running . . . he . . . he's dead." In the silence I dimly imagined her face.

"What? I didn't hear you." And I had to say it again.

I sat on a Louis XIV chair at a Louis XIV table which had been so visible, so important when we arrived; now everything I touched was black. My hand passed over the computer notebook with phone numbers Lance had given me. Had I complained it was unromantic? I remembered his laughter at my ingratitude. My fingers convulsed on it, as if I could hold onto him through it. I could hear his mother sobbing.

"Sheila?" No response. I waited for a long time. "Sheila? . . . It was this morning. He went for a run. It was very cold – it's autumn here, damp. He had a heart attack. They said it is dangerous to run early in the morning when it is cold. I hadn't known."

Still the sobs in the distance. I didn't know if she had even heard me. "I'll call again tomorrow."

I hung up and sat in a cold vacuum, as if she had sucked my grief down the wire and taken it for herself. After a minute of numbness, however, the pain returned. I got up and paced the room. Two fingers and the thumb of my right hand went to my wedding ring, wrapping along my finger. Memories began to taunt me: the music I associated with Lance before we got together, the images I collected of him to dream over, our first meal together, the wedding, his face, his smile, that squeeze of the hand that let me know he was aware of me when he seemed absorbed in something else, the future we had planned. I let them flicker past me again and again, trying to hold them even as they faded and I was left in the room alone. Then there was nothing but tears and the desperate thought: Please God, let me be pregnant.

Simon was waiting at the door, bags in his hands, but I couldn't leave this room, the last place I had touched him. I couldn't leave Lance behind. I buried my face again in his pillow, which I had sprayed with his cologne. It made him so real as I lay with my eyes shut that I had to tell myself again he was gone.

"Julia?"

"He's still here. How can I leave?"

Simon let the door close, put the bags down. His hair was dark instead of blonde and he was thinner, but there was an echo of Lance in the distinctive rose in the cheeks, the Cupid's bow mouth. He walked over to me, pulled me up from the bed and wrapped his arms around me. I pressed my face against his chest, seeking comfort but finding confusion as a different energy passed between us. I pulled away. "You're such a good friend. I know you miss him, too."

Simon looked away into a corner. I felt selfish, so wrapped up in myself I'd hardly thought about his grief.

11

"It can't be real. I close my eyes and I see him laughing."

"Describe it to me. Where is he?"

"In our tree house. He's ten, I'm eight. We've been dropping water bombs and he's just hit the neighbours' cat. He's triumphant, so real, so alive."

I smiled at the image.

"Then the last time we talked I was angry."

"Angry? Why?"

"Who knows? It doesn't matter now. I only wish . . ."

"What would you say to him, now, if you could?"

"I'd tell him I loved him, despite everything. I never told him - I guess brothers don't. But it's too late now. Come on, time to go."

"It reminds me of Dad," I said, in a small voice.

"What does?"

"Dad leaving. My dad left always in the same way. There one minute, and gone without saying."

Simon pulled me back to him. "It's okay. You'll be okay."

4

Their mother was at the airport when I arrived in Christchurch, jaded and dull. My movements had become minimal, conserving energy, and her violent hug shocked me. Before I could respond she let me go and I stumbled, covering it by reaching for my bag. Her eyes searched for mine, accusing, and I was bewildered by the concept of competitive grief.

We drove the ten minutes to her house in silence. I knew I should speak but I didn't know what she wanted to hear.

This house! The hedges and sweeping drive, I loved it, it was everything I had dreamed of in the card-house of my childhood. "You'll stay here, of course, until after the funeral."

"Thank you."

I expected the dream to twist into nightmare, but the banister under my hand was warm, enlivening. I had learned a lot about furniture, about architecture, since I was last here, and I soaked up details like a sapling taking food from the earth. This was home. I pressed down the minor key of Lance mocking in the background. "It's nothing. Just a house; just a place to grow up. You just live, it doesn't make any difference." But he had been wrong, it was only easy to dismiss if you had it.

"Put your bag in Lance's room and wash up. Then we'll have tea."

I closed the door of his room behind me and leaned against it, swallowing hard to stay calm. I had hardly seen it in the light before, assigned a guestroom on our pre-nuptial visit. Lance was dismissive: "No way, I won't sleep alone, with you down the hall." But I wanted to keep the peace, so I tiptoed in each evening and out before dawn. Lance laughed at my need to belong, used it as leverage to manipulate me the whole week we were here.

The mood in the room was complex: never-to-be-retrieved artefacts of Lance's childhood sat grumbling and chattering on shelves and desktop. The blue boyishness of it felt wrong, like Lance was slipping backwards in time towards his birth, back to his mother. It had never seemed less than grown up with him in it. I turned my back on the row of toy cars and aeroplanes and opened my bag. Shower, fresh clothes, get out of here.

I sat on the edge of my chair in the drawing room. Sheila looked me up and down. I don't think she ever thought I was good enough for him. "You've changed, less gauche. That was Lance, I suppose. Did he choose that jacket?"

I looked down, astonished. "Actually, yes."

She nodded approvingly. "You could wear it to the funeral. On that subject, there are a lot of decisions to make, are you up to it now?"

It was like she was planning a garden party: music, food, guest list. She was businesslike, with surreal interludes of noisy tears. I became more and more wooden; I had no idea how I was expected to behave.

"Is Simon here?"

"Arriving tonight. Now, flowers."

14

By the end it just flowed over me and I faded into a disconnected sadness, only dimly aware of the wetness on my cheeks. I stood, jetlag removing me further. "Do you mind if I sleep now?"

"What about dinner?"

"I just really need to sleep."

Sheila's lips pursed and I imagined a scoreboard, with me clicking one step closer to defeat.

I came in from a walk the next day to find my mother and Sheila sitting together. Mum's provincial beauty salon look was out of place in the formal room, which had the air of a duel, teacups at twenty paces: Sheila's little finger slanted elegantly out, her other hand cradling the saucer; Mum's whole fist held her cup like a captive bird and the saucer was abandoned on a table.

"Brenda has been waiting."

I felt protective. Mum's so straightforward; she's no match for Sheila.

"I'm so sorry. I wasn't expecting you until tomorrow." I moved between them and hugged her. She felt small and frail.

"I took the bus from Ashburton this morning. I wanted to see how you were."

"I'll leave you two to talk." Sheila stood and motioned me into her chair but I didn't want to let Mum go. I stayed standing, holding her by the arms.

"How are you, Mum, have you been okay?"

"I'm fine. Really. Things are good. But you . . ."

I turned my head away from the pity in her gaze, letting my hands fall and feeling for the chair behind me.

"How are you?"

I shrugged.

"What will you do? Do you want to come home?"

It took a moment to find an answer. I hadn't thought beyond today. "No. I'll stay in Christchurch, I guess. Find a job."

"And what do you plan to do? You were going to Wellington."

"Mum, that was before . . . I don't have any plans, I'm just . . ."

"Do you have friends you can stay with?"

"I suppose . . . I don't know."

"What about work? Do you have enough money?"

I stood up and paced behind the chair. Under the avalanche of questions I felt like a teenager again. "Mum, I don't know. I haven't thought about it. I suppose I'll look in the paper. Or my old company would probably have me back."

"You won't think about doing something different?"

"What do you mean?"

"Computers! It seems so dry."

I blew out a breath and walked faster, back and forth. "I can't think about it yet," I said, finally, sitting down again. Change the subject, get back to her. "You're still at the salon?"

"Yes."

I hesitated. "And how is Dad?"

"Quite well."

"How long since you've seen him?"

She looked away. "A few weeks."

16

"Or months?"

No reply.

"But you expect him back."

"He always comes back."

This hurt was so old. "But why, Mum? Why let him? I don't understand how you can keep on loving him when he keeps on doing this."

"I keep on loving him because that is what love is. It doesn't depend on what people do, or where they are. I'm happy even when he's not with me and I'm happier when he's there." She started defensive but ended with a radiant smile.

"I don't understand it."

"I know. That's why I think you need a job you'll enjoy."

I sighed and slumped. "Not now, Mum, not now."

5

On the morning of the funeral there was a lot of bustle, gloves and flowers and cars. Simon travelled with me and held my hand firm. Once the service started I felt trapped. All I heard of what was said was Lance's name, over and over again. I stared at one arbitrary point until a memory hit, then threw my glance somewhere else, as if throwing off the memory at the same time. Then I would hear his name again, a blow on a bruise.

At the house afterwards Simon and I stood apart from the crowd, people spilling outside onto the newly mown lawn. He was watching me closely but it was easiest to pretend not to notice. I sat on a low brick wall and gazed towards the milling guests.

"How's Sheila doing?" I asked.

"She's lost her favourite. She said she won't recover. And she's never wrong."

"She's got you."

"The shadow son." I was about to protest but he changed the subject. "That's your father?" He inclined his head towards a tall, broad man with thick, shoulder-length hair, who was engaging Sheila in conversation.

I raised my eyebrows and wrinkled my nose.

"He lectures maths, right?"

"Yeah."

"So why didn't we know? At university. You never told me. Did anyone know?"

I shook my head. "We're not close. He didn't live with us. Came and went like the sun on an autumn afternoon. Goodness knows how many children he has fathered in his walkabouts. And look at him now! Flirt." Sheila was laughing, relaxed, well out of character. Dad placed a hand on her arm and she put her other hand on his. I looked around for Mum, to see her reaction. She wasn't in sight.

Still watching him, I was disturbed when he looked up and caught me. He put his hand out to Sheila again, said something then moved towards me. Simon saw him coming and stepped away.

"Stay, I'll introduce you."

"It's not the time."

I braced myself.

"Julia."

"Dad."

He pulled me into a close hug and though I resisted for a moment I found myself melting into his embrace. "My poor darling." What was it about him? Tears flowed and I felt grief wash through me.

I pulled back. "Oh Dad! Why are you never here when I need you?" It was a ridiculous thing to say. Here he was, just when I did need him. "Does Mum know you're here?"

"She stayed with me last night."

It was so confusing, this thing they had which I couldn't understand.

"She said she hadn't seen you for months!" He shrugged. I felt so shut out. "I don't understand you!"

When I was five I learned to hold in the frustration, turn my shoulder against him and pretend the rejection was mine; then later I complained for Mum rather than for myself. I swayed, wanting to hit him.

"Just let me be here for you, now."

I gritted my teeth. "It's. Too. Late." I turned and walked back to the house, in search of Simon.

Two days later my period was due. It came. The grief was so intense I couldn't locate it. When I was 19 I jumped from a plane with a faulty parachute, landing badly and damaging my ankle. There was so much pain it took minutes to work out what hurt, before I could begin to move.

This was just like that, the same overwhelming level of distress. Was the grief for the baby I had dreamed of, or for the last thread of Lance? Whatever, I thought I would go insane. I walked out of the house, fast, becoming lost in my blind progress. At every corner I turned, sometimes doubling back on myself, shrieking with frustration when long into my contorted route I recognised Sheila's hedge and gate again, crossing the road to lose myself once more. I don't know what I did, what noise I made, if anyone saw me. I don't know how long I stayed away. Some time later I grew back into myself and found my way home. And I felt ashamed of the new grief I felt, walking back up the drive: a grandchild would have given me right of belonging, but this could not be my home now.

I packed my bag that afternoon, not knowing where I would go. Simon was leaving, too, going back to Cambridge, but before his flight I asked him to take me to the cemetery.

"What's up?"

As we drove out the gate I allowed my tears to spill over. It took a few attempts but finally my voice croaked out. "I thought I was pregnant. I'm not."

I saw him swallow as he took this in. He glanced over, then back at the road. "How do you feel?"

"Like a failure. Sad. Lonely."

"I hate seeing you like this. All the life's gone out of you. Shall I pull over? Do you want to talk?"

"We're talking, just drive." But instead of saying anything more, I leaned my head on the door pillar and cried until I had nothing left.

On the edge of Banks Peninsula the churchyard sat at the base of a hill, the green of native timber rising behind. It had been raining and the drops were wet on the grass, reflecting the sunshine in tiny flashes. There was no headstone on the grave; that would come later, Sheila's grand, unnecessary statement.

It felt peaceful now the crowd was gone. I spoke into the hope of the birdsong. "Please, Lance, won't you stay with me? I promise I'll never love anyone else the way I loved you. Just please stay."

6

Two months later

I rolled away from the window where the curtains, failing to meet, revealed a night sky tainted with streetlight orange. It was too early to wake. Damn! I pulled the pillow over my head but the heavy feathers moulded around my nose, suffocating. When was I going to stop feeling like this? I dragged the pillow away and raised my head again, groaning. I brought my feet up under my body and onto the floor.

The vinyl was cold on my soles as I walked around the bed to pull the curtains back. It was an effort to keep my eyes open; my throat was dry. I glanced towards the glass of water by the bed but stayed at the window. At least there was a faint hint of dawn in the sky.

Maybe I would go out. There might be some relief in the growing daylight. My hand went to my head. I should wash my hair, but there was no shampoo. Jeans, cardigan, cap. Out of habit I took my journal but I wrote in it less and less these days. The door clicked behind me.

I trod the neglected path without registering the cracks and weeds. The long driveway bordered the railway line and cycle path. An early cyclist swished past me, sucking air into a vacuum behind. It was too soon for the first passenger train, which would pass after seven. I pulled my collar close and hunched my shoulders. Just keep walking, change anything. I can't stay this way forever. Thoughts passed through my mind, unwelcome: a new anger at Lance for the life he had cost me. I had thought I would never be poor again. I closed my eyes and tried to hold onto the pure grief of missing him, absently crossing the tracks and walking along the road on the other side, ignoring dull 1970s houses and close-built units, before turning left towards Hagley Park and the city.

Wake up now. Road. Traffic. Glancing to my right I crossed the first half of the wide avenue then paused to allow a delivery van to pass before covering the next two lanes, jumping the low fence into the park. I took a diagonal line across the playing fields then entered the dark of the trees.

It was past time to find work but every time I thought about it I just wanted to sleep. I was good at my software job but it was never the life I wanted and survival wasn't enough of a reason any more. There were the careers I'd always dreamed of: creative, fun; but the thought of sparkling, selling myself, made my stomach sour.

I turned my attention to the sinister shadows of branches on the path, flinching as I unexpectedly emerged from their shade. The dawn was progressing. I followed the tram tracks on Armagh Street, crossed Cranmer Square to Salisbury Street and turned left into Victoria. Lights shone out from a café. Company. Distraction. I pushed the door open and felt the warmth embrace me.

A sleepy waitress was still setting up tables.

"Morning." Sliding back into a corner I took out my wallet. Hoping for more, I nevertheless found only the five dollar note I remembered. Two twenty cent coins and a ten. Just coffee then. Shame, I was suddenly hungry, and I had missed real hunger since . . . "How much for toast and jam?"

"Four fifty."

"Okay."

The girl stifled a yawn as she wrote the order.

"Late night?"

She looked up from her pad. "Nah! I am just SO not a morning person. What gets you up so early?"

I shrugged. "I suppose the dawn woke me."

"Dawn? What's that? I sleep on my way here, wake up around nine." She turned and called over her shoulder. "Hey, Carl, toast here, and set me up a coffee, would you?"

"Make it yourself, Donna, Christ!" He continued muttering; the girl laughed and shuffled over to the counter, yawning again as she turned on the grinder. The smell of coffee made me waver, but I needed food.

Donna delivered the toast and as I began to eat I pulled over the newspaper, checking the contents and turning to the Situations Vacant. I turned the pages without interest. Programmer, software engineer. Another advertisement caught my eye. "Bright, innovative person with creative flair sought for trainee position in design firm." A new kind of future flickered for a moment then died. I pushed the paper away and spread another piece of toast, closing my eyes, tasting the sweet jam and feeling the firm edges of the bread slide down my throat.

Donna walked past. "Want anything else?"

"You don't need another waitress, do you?"

"You want to work here?"

Why not? It would be easy. I wouldn't have to think much and it would keep me alive. "Yeah."

Donna didn't answer, just turned her head and called again over her shoulder. "Hey, Carl, do you need another waitress?"

Carl came out of the kitchen wiping his hands on his apron. He was large, stooped shoulders, face creased. "Who's asking?"

I turned on a smile; after weeks of tears it was like peeling back the lid of a soup can. "Me."

He beamed. "Ever waitressed before?"

"No."

"Well, you'll pick it up. Start tonight."

"Really?"

"See you at four."

7

For the first week I came home exhausted, grateful for the easy sleep that came after an evening of running, learning how everything worked. There was guilty relief in being too tired to think about Lance. Then I got used to the work and came through the door wide awake, needing to read until I wound down.

One Thursday, when there had been a particularly fun crowd in till late, I arrived home fizzing with excitement. I began pacing back and forth but instead of getting sleepy my eyes seemed wider open. I found myself really looking at the room around me. Things were everywhere, clothes draped over chairs and spread out on the cold side of the bed. I began tidying, straightening things, sorting out the mess, but soon everything was in place and still I was wired and restless. The peeling wallpaper caught my eye. I stood on the spot, eyes moving around the room, noticing the wide, ornate window seat, obscured by voluminous brown curtains, the large built-in cupboard, the lead-lights, the cornices, the ceiling rose and the cracked 1960s light fitting below it.

"That has got to go," I murmured aloud. I pulled over a plastic dining chair and stood up to remove it. The bare bulb swayed relatively inoffensively.

"Okay, let's go with it," and then I was moving furniture out of the room to wherever I could find space. The Formica table almost filled the little kitchen, the threadbare yellow sofa and chairs squashed into the bedroom, the coffee table leaned against the wall in the tiny entrance. I looked again at the cupboard and closed my eyes in distaste. It was thin, cheap and oddly placed in the room. I walked back to the bedroom, stared out the window, but seconds later I was back, peering around the sides to see how it was attached to the wall. A series of plates with screws held it on both sides, but it looked quite self-contained. I opened the doors and looked at the back, which was solid, not just open to the wall behind. Why would anyone bother to do that? I shrugged, finally beginning to feel sleepy. I'd think about it tomorrow.

In the morning my enthusiasm was back and I found myself at eight o'clock in a hardware store. Lots of tradesmen were around, picking up supplies for the day, but they knew what they were doing and the assistants were unoccupied. A young guy approached me, tall with dark curly hair, his face serious and practical. "Can I help you with anything?"

"Yeah, hi." I read his name badge. "Mark. How're you doing?"

He brightened. "Great. You?"

"Fantastic, getting excited about this project. I want to paint a room in my apartment, but I've never done it before. Where do I start?"

"Well, preparation. What's it like now?"

"Peeling, awful wallpaper, good bones, window seat."

"Hmm – the paper makes it harder."

"Tell me the worst, I can take it."

He talked me through removing the wallpaper, organised a hire steamer, wrote down what undercoats, fillers, tools I would need and sold me some dust sheets, brushes and rollers.

"Have you chosen a colour? The charts are over here. We have a colour consultant if you want advice."

"No, I'm fine with that, you've been a big help, that's fantastic."

Back in the apartment I stood in the middle of the room feeling slightly bewildered. Well, might as well just get going. Do the first obvious thing. I found old clothes, laid out the dust sheets in a corner by the window and sat down to work out the steamer. My lease said something about "no permanent changes", but what the hell, I couldn't make it any worse. I took a peeling corner between my fingers and deliberately tore it up the wall.

"No going back now."

8

A few days later, most of the wallpaper gone, I stood staring at the built-in wardrobe. I shrugged and began tidying up, clearing the last of the scraps into a rubbish bag, taking it out to the bins at the back of the house and catching snatches of the neighbours' shouted argument as I came and went through the hall. On my way back I stopped to investigate a cupboard under the stairs – nothing in it but a couple of broken banister rails.

A door banged on the landing. "I'm glad to get out! Bitch!" The neighbours' huge, scary dog dragged its owner down the stairs at full speed.

"Hi." I tried to catch his eye as they passed, but the man didn't respond. Upstairs there was quiet for a moment, then an explosion of music thrashing through the walls. Great. I went back into my apartment but the noise diminished only slightly when I closed the door behind me.

I looked at the ugly, scratched coffee table and faded, clichéd prints I had stacked in the entrance, picked them up and took them out to the hall. The stairs were wide and the space under them was huge. I carried everything to the far corner and put them there where the ceiling was low under the first treads. A few more trips took care of every ugly thing I could live without and I stood in the living room again feeling lighter. Just that cupboard. Maybe there were some tools in the kitchen – but no. Shame, I was pretty sure it would only take a screwdriver . . .

Back at the hardware store I was waiting at the checkout when Mark came over to talk.

He grinned shyly. "How did it go? Did the wallpaper come off okay?"

"Yeah, fine. I'm just returning the steamer. Thanks a lot for your advice, it was brilliant!"

Mark ducked his head down. "Nah, no problem, glad to help. Here, I'll take that." He put the steamer to one side. "Just the screwdriver today? Something need fixing?"

"Sort of." I explained about the cupboard. "I'm pretty sure I can take it off by myself. I'll worry about how to get it out of the apartment later, it's huge."

"Do you need a hand shifting it? Where are you going to take it?"

"Not far - are you offering?"

Mark hesitated, then, "Yeah, sure, I could come round after work. Where do you live?"

It was more firmly attached than it looked and several chunks of wall came away with the plates, which seemed to be glued as well as screwed on. We were just manoeuvring it towards the door when there was a shout from the hallway.

I stared at Mark, eyes wide, half laughing, half horrified. "What?" he whispered.

"Oh hell, it's the landlord. Wait here, quietly, and if he comes in, stand in front of it."

"What? Weren't you supposed to . . ." I picked up an envelope from the mantelpiece and slipped out the door, closing it behind me.

"If I don't have it by Monday you're out!" he was shouting ineffectually at the door on the landing.

"Hi, Hunter, how are you?" I started up the stairs as he turned. His face morphed quickly from angry bastard to would-be gallant. He leaned on the rail, prepared to charm.

"Julia, my dear, what a delight!"

"Here's the rent." I leaned across from the stairs to hand him the cash, which he glanced at and then pocketed.

"You're so easy." The word hung in the air, suggestive. I tilted my head, daring him to follow it up. "I mean, I wish all my tenants were like you. Those wastrels haven't got the rent again."

"Well, variety is the spice of life, Hunter." There was a thump from my apartment and I smiled more agreeably than I intended, to cover it. Hunter took a step or two down the stairs towards me.

"Any chance of a coffee? My wife's premenstrual and I'm longing for a kind word." He leaned closer, his eyes comically hopeful.

"Actually, Hunter, I have someone here," I whispered. "Maybe another time."

"Okay." He pouted. "See you in a fortnight." He leered a parting grin and I slipped back into the apartment as he closed the front door. I put a finger to my lips as Mark began to speak and went to the window. Hunter walked down the path, counting the rent, tripping on a loose flagstone. The lights flashed on his chick-magnet car and he opened the door.

I let the curtain fall back out of my hand. "Okay, let's go."

9

I felt alive as I worked, hands occupied, thoughts free. Life was good – enough social life at the café and in the daytime the creative satisfaction of this project. As I got near the end I looked at the furniture. The sofas could be covered with throws, the chest of drawers was okay. What I couldn't stand I either replaced with second-hand pieces I stripped back or painted, or did without.

The joy of finishing the apartment was intense. I stood in the doorway and was amazed to see my vision, here in front of me, made real. I went to the window, looked out at the overgrown garden, turned back into the room and laughed.

"I've finished!" I shouted down the phone to Nora, who worked with me at the café.

"Great! . . . Finished what?"

"The flat! Painting! Everything! Let's go out and celebrate!"

"Good idea, except for one thing: we're both due at work in an hour."

"Oh, yeah. Well then, after that?"

Work that night was over before I looked up. My mood annoyed Donna, though she tried to hide it. "What are you on, girl?" she whispered as she passed me, as I was laughing with a customer.

"What is she on?" she repeated to Nora.

"She's excited because she finished painting her apartment."

"That's all? I thought she must have won the lottery."

I came up behind and put an arm around each of them. "Don't you just love them?"

"Who?" asked Donna, a challenge in her voice.

"The customers! They're just great, out having fun. I love it!"

"They look the same as always to me," Donna answered dryly.

Nora whooped as she counted the tips. "You should be like this every night, Julia, this is twice what we've ever had before!"

Donna and I were setting up tables for the morning.

I grinned. "Hey, I'm really not ready to go home. Midnight stroll?"

Nora frowned. "I have an essay to write tomorrow, it's already late."

Donna rolled her eyes. She kept up a tough girl façade but there was deep warmth if you could get her to relax. "Okay Miss Girly Swot! Go on, don't rain on her parade." She pulled off her apron to reveal a cut-off top and low jeans.

I watched Nora, her movements small and constrained. She was a university student in the Gothic tradition, black clothes, straight dark hair, thin, with a slightly uncared-for look. "I'd love you to come. Go over there, make a start on your essay. We'll finish up."

"Okay."

We walked on the sand. The waves were gentle, just enough to break up the river of the moon's reflection. I stopped and gazed out over the ocean. "I just feel so free, like anything is possible! I saw it and I made it come true. It's like there's this huge blank canvas and I can fill it with anything I want."

Donna grunted and carried on walking. "Damn. I've got sand in my shoes."

I ran to catch up with her. "Take them off then, Donna, feel the sand on your feet."

"I can already feel the sand on my feet, in my shoes." But she stopped to untie her laces.

"There might be broken glass."

"Nora!"

"Sorry."

"Live a little - I keep telling you!" Donna sneered, but I put my arm around Nora's shoulder.

"We love you the way you are, you know that . . ."

A few steps further on I stopped and looked out to sea. An unwelcome melancholy came in waves, the spill of the grief I usually kept at bay with activity. Should I tell them about Lance? No, not now, this was supposed to be a celebration.

"Let's go for a swim." I turned to the others and began to strip off my clothes.

"But . . . but . . ."

"Come on!" I started towards the water.

"It'll be cold."

"Yes, come on, a chance to feel something more than everyday."

Nora hesitated, then began taking off her shoes.

"You, too, Donna."

"Uh-uh. Too cold for me."

"Live a little," Nora mimicked, but still Donna refused, so we plunged in together. I thought my heart would stop at the shock of the water. My breath came in laughing spasms. I swam strong, smooth strokes towards the moon, until Nora called me back. We floated on the gentle waves, looking up at the sky.

I let my lungs empty in a slow sigh, sinking. "Feel the world getting bigger?"

"What do you mean?"

"Every time I do something I haven't done before, it's like more possibilities open up." I was speaking more to myself as I continued. "I hate feeling, ever, that there is something I can't do. Sometimes I have to force myself to be brave. But I'm afraid, if I'm not . . . life shrinks to become a cage."

There was a pause as Nora considered the idea. "Am I a coward?"

"You? That's not what I meant, look where you are, naked in public, submerged in body-numbing water, discussing philosophy. Now there," I raised my voice and splashed towards the beach, "is a coward."

"I'm just not crazy," Donna answered, shading her eyes from the moonlight and peering into the darkness. "Come out, I'm getting cold standing around here."

"She's getting cold," I remarked.

"Poor thing." Nora began to wade out of the water. "Let's get her." We ran across the beach, launching ourselves at her and knocking her to the ground. Sand slid across my skin and stuck in contour patterns.

"Get off me," Donna laughed. "You're all wet! Get off!"

10

The next Monday morning there was worse shouting than usual from upstairs. I was feeling low and for a moment was glad of the distraction. I went out into the hall to see if I could help, but when I got there, Hunter was storming and raging on the landing on his own. Nathan, from the apartment above mine, had come out, too, to see what was happening. I caught his eye then went to Hunter and put a hand on his arm. "What's the matter?"

"They've gone, they've fucking gone, paid no rent and they've taken everything." I looked through the open door and saw he was right, the place was empty. I turned to Nathan.

"Did you know about this?"

"No. They must have gone while I was at work."

I stepped through the door and looked around, involuntarily stopping my breath. The dog had obviously spent its days peeing on the walls and carpet, there were stains on the floor and the paper was peeling horribly at the bottom. And there was nothing: no light fittings, curtains, pictures, it was bare. Hunter had stopped shouting and when I turned around I was appalled to see he was crying. I gestured Nathan away, put a hand on Hunter's shoulder and took him down to my apartment.

He was too generally insensitive to his surroundings and too upset to notice the changes. I made him coffee and let him talk out his annoyance and frustration, thinking quickly. This looked like the opportunity I had been hoping for. When he had finished and begun to repeat himself I asked him how much rent they had owed, how much he thought the furniture was worth. It wasn't as bad as I had feared, and he was probably overestimating the value of the contents. He clearly hated losing anything, but seemed calmer once he had put a number on it.

I took a breath. "I've got an idea; maybe this is a blessing in disguise. Look around you. I've been working on this place and it's looking great." Hunter lifted his head. I watched nervously as he took in the improvements. This was my chance.

"What if I did the same upstairs? Take my word for it, you can ask double the rent for this place now. I'll move out, and sell you some of the furniture to go with it. The location is fantastic, but you've lost good prospects because of the way it looked - it will rent in a day, you'll get better tenants, all good news." My speech accelerated. "I'll move into the bigger apartment, do the same thing with it and when I go you'll get more for that as well. I could do the apartments in turn, plus the entrance hall and stairs need work. You pay the costs - I'll keep them as low as possible - and leave the rest to me."

I could see the idea slowly revolving in his mind, out of place among his usual preoccupations of sex and resentment. I had lost him fairly early on in my explanation, so I would have to go over the details again later, but now I waited for his reaction.

"It sounds like a good idea." Hunter frowned, thinking. "But can you afford the extra rent?"

Uh-oh, we'll have to take it slow here. I leaned across the table and looked him in the eye. "Rent-free, Hunter. Work in exchange for rent."

This was harder for him to understand, but finally, with repetition, he was convinced he would be better off than before, even in the short term, and he agreed.

I took the fortnight's rent I had had ready for Hunter and bought an antique lamp I had seen and loved. It felt so good to do something so self-indulgent.

I took photographs of the upstairs apartment so that once I was done I could compare Before and After. I took some of my current apartment, too. Then I began work. At least there wasn't any furniture to carry out this time.

Pulling up the carpet was a foul job, but it made a good story when I went to work that evening. Being upstairs, the wood was plainer, straight boards instead of parquet, but it would still work well. I scrubbed the floor several times to make sure the smell was completely gone and left it bare while I steamed the paper off the walls, pulled out more cheap, built-in furniture and thought about what I would do. This moment was magical, when I could see the future unfolding like a landscape emerging from fog. The dreary details receded and fresh scenes took their place. The work was easy when I saw so clearly where I was going.

Sanding the large living room was a big task but in a few weeks the floor was done, the walls were ready for painting and I moved in. It was strange leaving my first apartment – Hunter already had a tenant waiting. I stood in the doorway as I left it, trying to remember what it had been like. A surging sense of achievement made me laugh out loud.

11

Hunter had set a budget for the renovation. I hated haggling and Hunter was a master at it, but if I was careful it would be enough. I needed a bed, lounge furniture, some lamps, curtains, as well as paint; the bathroom would be expensive, but I had some ideas that would make the kitchen cheaper.

Nora came shopping with me. For now I just needed a mattress; the rest could come later. Carl had recommended a cheap bed shop, but even the economy dense-foam mattress I chose emptied my bank account. "I hope Hunter pays up quickly, or I'll be eating spaghetti out of a tin for a long time." Delivery was arranged for the next day and we wandered back towards the City Mall.

Nora paused outside an art shop. "Maybe I should have studied art instead of English."

"You still could."

"No, this is my last year, I can't start again." She looked wistfully at the pictures in the window.

"Let's go in," I suggested.

"They'll know we can't afford . . ."

"We can look, come on, it's fine."

I swept my eyes along one wall then started flipping through a stack of pictures leaning piled up. Nora came up next to me and I whispered over my shoulder. "Well, they're expensive, but I don't like many of them very much. Do you?"

Nora looked around the shop. "What about that one?" She pointed to a wide, empty landscape, sunlight playing through patchy dark cloud to form a pattern of golden glow.

I considered for a moment, then nodded. "The prices seem worse when you do like them." I took Nora's arm and steered her out. "I'll get some old movie posters – they're always cool."

We found a cheap wicker chair in a second-hand shop, put it aside to pick up once Hunter had paid me and went to the hardware store to buy paint. Hunter had agreed to meet me there at twelve, but as we walked through the door my mobile rang.

"Julia, hi, listen, I'm tied up at the moment. Can you get the paint and I'll pay you back?"

"I've already paid for the mattress, there's nothing left."

"Can it wait until tomorrow?"

"I'd rather get going. And I'm here now."

There was a pause. "Ok, I'll be down in half an hour."

"Listen, I know it's a pain. Maybe you could put some of the budget in my bank account, then I wouldn't have to call you out all the time." I pulled a face at Nora, stretching out my mouth and rolling my eyes.

"No. No. I'll be there."

"Half an hour!" I complained when I had hung up.

Nora laughed. "Julia's legendary patience!"

"Let's see if Mark's free."

Mark was at lunch but one of the other assistants called him down. "I'm painting tonight, but come over? See the new apartment and we can go out afterwards."

Mark grinned.

"What's happening there, J?" Nora asked, after he had gone back to his sandwiches.

"Nothing serious, but it's fun, he's a nice guy. Don't look at me like that, you should know me better. Besides, they won't have delivered the mattress before tonight."

Nora looked at me sideways "I'm never sure whether you're serious or not."

Hunter arrived forty-five minutes later; I hate waiting, I was wearing out the pavement, but I put on a bright smile for him. Got to keep him sweet.

He promised to put the money for the mattress into my account that day and disappeared without helping to carry the paint to the car, which was parked outside a café a couple of shops away.

"Let's have lunch," Nora suggested as she closed the boot.

"No cash."

"My shout." She looked at the menu for a moment but then put it down. "I've been thinking."

"Yes?"

"About what you said, about being brave."

"Yes?"

"The thing is, how do you decide what to be brave about?"

"Do I sound so full of answers? My own life has been pretty random."

"But you said when you're brave, more possibilities open up. So what are you brave about?"

I looked around the room, absently taking in the materials and colours on the walls, corrugated iron and deep rich browns, with large white pictures. "I'm not sure what to tell you. I'm brave about the physical things, like the apartments. It means I can do more of what I enjoy, and once I'm doing that I see more clearly what I want to do. I take opportunities as they come, I don't necessarily plan it out beforehand, but then once I'm in a project it all becomes clear. It's fun." I paused. "And then sometimes I think all that activity is just to avoid the other things, relationships, love, the things I'm scared of."

"You? Scared?"

"Yeah."

"So what about the traditional life: family, husband, children, security. Does that fit in or not?"

"I'd love it to, but I don't trust it, and I don't think I could stand the hurt if it went wrong again."

"Again?"

I ignored the question. "Anyway, I wonder if it feels the same inside as it looks from the outside."

Nora looked thoughtful. I took advantage of the pause to change the subject. "Shall we order? I want to get back and start work."

12

I loved painting. As I became more skilled at it I enjoyed it more, the whole picture filling my head as I focused on each detail. For the grand, classical architecture I stayed with a simple colour theme: cream, with antique gold accents. I spent hours on the ladder applying the thin metallic paint to the picture rail, surprised how the many wobbles with the tiny brush were invisible from the ground.

With the physical work my thoughts became sharper, ideas flowed fast and formed themselves into ambitious plans, short-term and long-term, plans for the apartment, the house, my future and my life – guiltily pleased at not having to consider anyone else.

Hunter was slippery, reluctant to part with his money. I was often down to nothing, only eating properly at the café after work. It got harder and harder to be civil to him.

I saw Mark every week or so, very casual. I kept thinking he was everything Lance would have despised. Lance himself, and the life I might have been living I repeatedly pushed out of my mind; but I couldn't keep him out of my dreams.

I became aware of my surroundings everywhere I went, and of details I had previously ignored: the way the proportions of a room affected acoustics and airflow, how I hated to be in a room that was too well sealed. The solidity of the walls was something I could sense now without having to tap on them to know whether they were sound or flimsy. I looked at shops, restaurants, theatres, offices, friends' houses, anywhere I found myself. Magazines were interesting but real spaces taught me more. I made notes, of new facts and the ideas that came from them; I watched light, came to despise dark curtains, which obstructed the light even when pulled open.

I noticed how a glimpsed view, to another room, or outside, made me feel curious, but closed doors, excluding, annoyed me. I began to match the outside of a building to the inside, to be able to guess what I would find, to learn from what was common and what surprised. I became aware of how an intriguing feature on the outside - bay window, balcony, stairwell - could be much less significant inside, and thought how it could be made a feature here, too. I filled notebooks with my observations and my understanding grew into structured thought and analysis; I drew pictures and sketched more formal plans in larger books.

The apartment progressed, developing in much the same way as the first. The walls were finished, and this time I picked out the details around windows, picture rails, coving and ceiling mouldings in deeper shades as well as the touches of gold. The kitchen was bigger than the first one, with room to play. I took a deep breath and pulled all the old cupboards out. Mark's brother made a built-in breakfast table and banquette I had designed for the bay window, which I stained and varnished, tying on cushions I had covered with a remnant of half-price brocade. My living room was a workshop.

I spent time in second-hand shops, looking for cupboards, drawers and something I could have a sink put into. Old painted wood was easiest to find. Some of it I stripped and varnished, hot work but easy to fit into the time I had available – I could do it in short bursts, even on the days I worked lunch and evening in the café.

When the wood turned out to be lower quality, or mismatched, or not well assembled, I painted the pieces, experimenting with colours, mostly creams to tone with the wood, but here and there adding detail or allowing a stronger colour to show through an artificially worn surface.

New sinks and taps were terrifyingly expensive but I was delighted to find a good choice in a salvage yard. I found a big porcelain basin with the original taps still in it, which would look fantastic in the old mahogany desk I had bought. The top was badly marked, but the worst bit would be cut out. It would be a quirky sink unit: cheap, but full of character. I sanded it and applied several coats of marine polyurethane, extra on the top.

Hunter insisted we use his friend, Vico, as plumber, creepy, leering and half-drunk at 9 in the morning. Presumably he was cheap. With a combination of close supervision and flattery the job was adequately done, and I cut the hole for the basin myself.

"Sure you know what you're doing there, Love?"

It wasn't a huge job, the pipes connecting to where the old ones had been. Once it was finished we moved another piece of furniture in next to it and it was like magic.

"Wow!"

"Unusual, but very effective." Vico surveyed it proudly, as if he'd thought of it himself. I slipped sideways to avoid his hand as he attempted to slap my bottom.

It was rent day and Hunter dropped in as usual, to leer and chat and complain. He only had two apartments to collect from now, since the single academic who had fallen in love with my first apartment paid by direct credit, a month in advance.

"I told you you'd get better tenants. Come and see the kitchen."

Hunter looked around, his face a dull mask of confusion.

"Don't you think it's great?!"

"Unusual, isn't it?" He was silent for a moment. "But I don't really see what was wrong with it before."

I sighed. "Not to worry, Hunter, it didn't cost much and the proof will be in the rent."

His eyes gleamed. "So you think I'll get twice as much again? How long will it be?"

"More than twice, because you'll actually get paid. And be patient, the bathroom's still to do. I'll go back to the scrap yard for the basin, and get the bath resurfaced . . ." We walked through and looked at it, rolled top and claw feet. "I can paint the outside myself . . . but we need a new loo."

Hunter began to protest.

"Need, I said, no option . . . and I think I'll find someone else to do it, Vico's not . . ."

Hunter shook his head, nervous. His voice was intense. "Vico's cheap, and he's a mate, and . . ."

"Okay, okay, calm down. Have some coffee, or open the wine you brought."

Hunter drank the wine and began to mellow. He was in the right mood for the next suggestion. "Once the bathroom's finished, I'll be ready to move. Nathan's flat's not bad, I can move straight in, but I don't want to start it yet, I want to do the hall next, and stairs. The floor will be a feature of the house and the banisters and rails just need stripping. The walls are high, I'll need help to paint them, and I want to put a skylight where the roof slopes over the landing."

Hunter gasped. "How much will it cost?"

"I've worked it out. $7,000, all up, painting included."

"$7,000!"

"Calm down. How much extra rent are you getting for my old flat and how much will you for this one? It's a few months' extra, just from these two. It has to be done, no question. And this time I want access to the money at the start. I've been cutting my hours at work to paint, I can't be covering the expenses, even temporarily."

Hunter's face went red.

I condensed months of financial frustration into sharp, clear words. "That's the deal. You'll just have to trust me."

LAW OF ATTRACTION

13

Nora and Donna came over for brunch, Nora cooing over the flat, Donna quiet.

"Come into the kitchen. I'm making pancakes." As I cooked I watched Donna, arms wrapped around her knees, staring out the window. She had broken up with her boyfriend a few weeks before but had said very little about how and why. Nora slid onto the banquette in the bay window and propped her elbows on the table. Donna leaned into her hot-pink handbag and took out a cigarette.

"Move over," she ordered. Nora shuffled along and Donna opened the window, holding the cigarette in her mouth while she hunted for a lighter, sighing and pulling the bag from the floor onto her knee to look deeper.

I threw her a box of matches.

"Thanks."

Donna closed her eyes over a long inhale, then held her hand through the window, leaning back to exhale cleanly along the line of her arm. She sat up straighter and looked around for the first time. "Kitchen looks good," she said. "But what about that stove? Aren't you going to get a new one?"

I turned from a just-flipped pancake and feigned disbelief. "This? This is vintage! Freestanding, enamel. They don't make them like this any more."

"Yes, they do, just no-one with any taste buys them. That thing's a dinosaur!"

"Well, you can just shut up. I spent hours cleaning it, it's like new, and I think it looks fab . . . Besides, Hunter would collapse at the knees if I suggested a new one. I have to be pragmatic, only spend where it will really count. Damn, Hunter and money. He's really pissing me off." I took a deep breath and blew it slowly out of my nose. Forget it, think about something positive. "Have I told you about the stairs?"

I always love describing my plans, painting the picture of how things will be and I got carried away with the captive audience. It was only when I poured another coffee that I slowed down, then paused to laugh at myself. Nora was relaxed and smiling. Donna yawned and stretched out like a cat, nudging Nora further along the banquette.

"I don't know where you find the energy." Her voice was muffled behind the table. "Eddy moved in, by the way."

Nora and I stared at each other.

"The guy you met the other night?"

"Good grief, that was quick! What's he like?"

"Oh, you know, strong, silent, that occasional mean glint in his eye which I can never resist. Energetic in bed. Perfect, really."

"For goodness sake, sit up so we can see you." I leaned over and poked her in the stomach. She lazily propped herself up on one elbow. "Why didn't you bring him this morning?"

"Yes, why? We want to meet him properly."

"Well, I guess I . . ." there was something she wasn't saying, something competitive in her eyes. "I guess I want to keep him to myself a bit longer, till he's properly hooked." She lay back down again. "Now would you let me rest? We were at it all last night."

I shrugged at Nora; there was nothing obvious to say. "Let's leave her. Come with me." I wanted to show her what I had been doing. We walked through the living room, sparsely furnished with salvaged pieces I had painted to match. "That's the dresser we found at the second-hand shop, remember? I want to find more pieces to paint. The furniture can move with me – the more I look around, the more I see expensive places tend to be let unfurnished, but for my portfolio I need enough furnishings for the photographs."

"Portfolio?"

"You know, I'm keeping a record, Before and After. But I can move bits from one room to another – it will add continuity, a uniformity of style. I'll go around the second-hand shops again soon, to see if I can find another lounge suite I can cover up."

We walked out onto the landing. "I can't wait to get started out here, I can just see it. It looks okay now, but it's dingy, let me show you the boards." At the bottom of the stairs I picked up a corner of the carpet. "See, parquet." I pulled it back a little bit further.

"It changes there, look." Nora pointed.

"Hey, yeah!" I tugged hard, tacks popping as I pulled back a big corner.

"Look, it's edged all around with a different pattern."

I laughed with delight. "It's inlaid wood – fantastic! Let's see how far it goes." And we kept pulling until one strip of carpet was removed, then started on the next. We carried the carpet outside. When we came back the downstairs tenant had the door open, scratching his head. "We didn't wake you, did we?" I asked, smiling as the door banged shut. "Three months and they'll be gone – I'm leaving that one till last, it's the best and I'm hoping to be left in it."

There was no reason to stop. Nora was excited, too. We cleared the floor and walls, me shouting my satisfaction as the faded Constable prints hit the rubbish pile. I put some broken stair rails on the porch with the furniture and we continued pulling up carpet, more carefully, removing tacks with the back of a hammer. Eventually Donna surfaced, grumbling. "Why didn't you wake me? I'm on lunch, I'll be late." But she didn't hurry, paused to stare at the mess, then wandered out and down the path.

"You go, too, Nora, if you like. I can finish here."

"No, it's fun, let's keep going."

The edging went all the way around, in and out of every corner and looked like it continued up the stairs.

"I wonder what wood this is, it's much lighter than the rest."

In the centre of the hall was a circular pattern in the same light wood. I stood in the doorway, excited, seeing not what was in front of me, but how it would be when it was finished. "Fantastic."

Nora nodded. I put a sweaty arm on her shoulder.

"See up there, how it's dark on the landing? Mark's brother is going to put in a skylight . . . I'll phone him today."

Three weeks later the floor was finished and the skylight was in. In my mind I already saw it completed but there was still the painting to do.

I had taken time out to find a basin, choose a toilet, paint the bath and organise Vico the plumber to get it all working, so the flat I had been living in was finished.

Nathan from the other upstairs apartment had been given notice so that I could start on that one. I felt a twinge of guilt as I saw him packing and helped him carry some things out to the car, then stood at the window and watched him go before moving my things across the landing.

Now I had too much furniture. This flat was above the first one and not much bigger. Some of the old furniture I could use, so I piled up the pieces I brought with me in the tiny bedroom and I would sleep for now in the lounge.

Tenants were found for the big flat but they didn't move in until the stair rail had been dismantled, stripped and put back in place. Once varnished and in the light from the new window it glowed golden.

I reduced my hours at the café for a while to spend more time working on the house, knowing it wasn't to my advantage to finish sooner but too caught up to slow down. Richard, the painter, was sixty and grandfatherly. He charged by the hour so it was cheaper if I helped. I loved working with him, and he taught me how to get a smooth, fast line when cutting in; the best order to paint the various surfaces; and how to wrap rollers in plastic food wrap and stand enamel paint brushes in water to save time cleaning up at the end of the day and getting started the next.

"It's amazing working with you," I told Richard, "turning to do something and finding you've already done it."

I lifted my brush from a last detail and looked up to see him grinning. We had finished. I ran to hug him, then we stood in the doorway and looked up. "Well done, Missy, that's a grand job."

I called Donna. "Let's go dancing tonight. I've got energy to burn. Bring that boyfriend we never see."

I spent most of the night on the dance floor, standing at the table to drink when I got thirsty.

"My muscles ache, but I've just got to keep moving."

Mark threw himself into a chair near where Nora was sitting. "Come on, get up!" I begged her. "You can't just watch all night! Mark, take Nora out for a dance." Nora allowed herself to be led into the crowd but five minutes later was back, safely observing again.

I felt a glow all evening, closing my eyes and seeing my achievement, but also absorbed in the music, the lights, the movement. At midnight Donna and Eddy left: Donna laughing, Eddy brooding.

I sat down next to Nora. The music was quieter now. Mark sat, too. Mid-sentence I glanced up at him and something made me freeze. What had made me think of Lance?

I stared at Mark, the angle of his head, the expression on his face, simple pleasure, and followed his eyes to where a pretty young girl was dancing on her own.

Mild disgust rose and fell again. I wasn't really surprised, or even offended, but it was time to disentangle myself.

He turned back to me and took my hand, I squeezed his in return. Better tell him tonight.

14

I found it difficult to get to sleep then woke with a jolt from a disturbing dream, Lance's mocking laughter echoing around the unfamiliar room. There was no light near the bed; I stood up and groped my way towards the door to find the switch. I had begun removing picture hooks as soon as I had moved my stuff into the new apartment, and the open toolbox tripped me. I fell against the wall. "Damn!" By the time I got the light on, my heart was beating fast. I'd never get back to sleep now.

The faded kitchen vinyl was sticky on my feet. I didn't blame Nathan for not cleaning properly, but my nose wrinkled. All my crockery and glassware was standing on the bench waiting for the cupboards to be wiped out. I filled a glass with water, looked around the room and shuddered. It would be better in the morning. A few hours cleaning and removing ugly things would transform the feeling of the place. Now, however, I felt cold and alone. 3:15. A long time till dawn.

Back in the living room I picked up a book and put it down again, considered starting the cleanup now - no. I really wanted to talk to someone about my nightmare, but who would understand? Not Donna or Nora, they still didn't know about Lance. Not Mum. A clear picture of my father's sympathetic face hung before me. I knew he would understand. For a moment my heart tugged that way, but I couldn't let him think I had forgiven him. Simon. Yes, Simon. He knew Lance's dark side as well as I did. And I wouldn't have to wake him, he'd be at work, in the middle of his afternoon.

"Simon? It's Julia. Are you busy, can you talk?"

"Just a minute." I heard him murmuring in the background, then he came back on the line. "Hey, how are you?"

The joy in his voice lifted me and I laughed. "Oh, you know, great, in general, but just at the moment sitting in the dark feeling sorry for myself. Sorry it's been so long since I rang."

"Me, too. But I think of you, every day."

"Yeah."

"So why are you feeling sorry for yourself?"

"Just a nightmare, nothing really."

"Tell me."

"Well . . . I can't remember much, but Lance – when I dream of him I never see him, just hear his voice – anyway, he was laughing at me, for thinking I could tie him down. 'You never really thought I'd be faithful, did you?' But silly. I don't know where it came from."

"Well, we all know he was a cad. But so did he. It was part of his charm." Simon didn't sound charmed, however. I knew he and Lance had argued about it more than once.

"Well, it's nothing, just a bad dream. Tell me about you. I just want to hear a friendly voice."

"I'm glad you called me." He talked about his work: starting as a computer programmer he was now running a team with a new project due to start in a few weeks. "But listen, I've got an idea. I've been thinking about it for a while." He hesitated. "I'm kind of done here. I loved Cambridge, and I enjoy the weekends in Europe, but I'm really over the English thing now. I'm ready for home. I think we may be able to do this new project there. I'll talk to my boss, come back for a trip, see if it can work."

"That would be great! I'd love to see you."

"Yeah, me too."

"Will you stay with Sheila?" I held my breath. I'd never see him if he did.

"No freedom. I'll get a flat."

"Are you crazy? You can stay here, with me." I looked around with new enthusiasm. "I'll have it looking great."

"Fantastic! I'll let you know when I've booked a flight."

The café was busy with a lively lunchtime crowd. I was dancing and the customers were chatty. Nora stopped outside the kitchen, a plate in hand.

"Julia, help, this guy says these aren't a 'true julienne, they're not nearly fine enough', but I can't tell Carl, he's frantic and angry enough already."

I took the plate and headed back out. "It's Harry. I'll deal with it. Take my order out for me?"

"Harry, what's the problem?" I whispered in his ear. Harry was fat, smug and pompous and I knew he'd love my breath on his face. He looked up and smoothed his vibrant pink and yellow tie over his stomach.

"Well . . ." he began, but I did not have time for his pace of speech.

I crouched down beside him. "Harry, physical description aside, how do the vegetables taste?" He sneered. "Go on, try them."

He took a reluctant bite.

"Well?" I prompted.

"All right, I suppose."

"Great, I'll tell Carl not to worry, and remember, ask me, don't rely on what the menu says, I'll tell you exactly what to expect. You're a honey not to mind this time."

He sneered again, this time an attempt at seduction. I stood up. "One day, we'll start a restaurant together and get these things right, okay?" His eyes lit up and he opened his mouth, but I turned away before he could speak.

"Thanks," whispered Nora.

"I'm so jazzed today, nothing can go wrong."

"What?"

"Just life." Someone across the café gestured at their watch. "I think I'll give Carl and Angie a hand, they're getting behind."

"I wouldn't go near, he's a ticking bomb."

But I went into the kitchen and kissed him. He threw up his hands then pointed. "Those just need garnish, but we've run out."

There was a pot of basil on the windowsill. I put generous sprigs on the plates. Carl rolled his eyes. "Okay, yes," and I was out the door.

Simon tried to slip in quietly but I was across the room before the door closed. As I threw my arms around him I felt tears in my eyes.

"It's so good to see you!" He didn't speak. "Well, hug me! Tighter." He hesitated, then pulled me close to him. My lips were on his neck. "I'm so glad you've come." I pulled away. He took off his sunglasses and I looked into his green eyes, pushing his dark hair back off his forehead. "Hey, you've put on some muscle, no more scrawny academic! It suits you. You look – I don't know – comfortable, successful."

"Older, you mean?"

"Well, but in a good way, and bigger, you used to sometimes look like you might disappear – I love the jacket, so grown up!"

He began to speak then stopped and started again. "How are you?" He peered closely into my face. "Missing Lance, huh?"

The words caught me in the chest, winding me. "Not now," I whispered. I cleared my throat. "Let me get you lunch, another hour and I'm off."

15

"Where shall we go? I have to be back by six."

Simon looked at his watch. He seemed nervous. "I have a car, shall we go for a drive?"

I took his hand as we walked up the street and his fingers tensed. I swung his arm then let go and turned to dance backwards in front of him, willing him to relax. He stopped walking and I stepped toward him.

"It is so lovely to see you, I can't say."

He swallowed. There was a moment's pause, then he reached into his pocket. A silver convertible next to us blipped.

"This? Oh wow! Can we have the top down? It's fantastic."

"You know I always wanted to be a flashy bastard. Time to start, I think, or I'll be too old for it to look good."

We drove out of town. Once I started to talk I couldn't stop. I told him everything I'd been doing, then ran from subject to subject, words bubbling up like a spring.

The road began to wind up a valley. I looked up at the hills and the sky, and stretched.

"Pull over, I need to touch you, make sure you're real."

I put my hand on his face. The muscles in his cheek tensed and for a moment I drank in the love in his eyes. He looked away.

"Do you know how often I wished I hadn't introduced you?"

"Simon!"

"I have to say something. I just need to get it out, so I'm not always watching my words." He looked back at me, asking for permission. I waited. He looked out the window again, at the distant view. "I cursed myself over and over again. He had you, and I wanted you so much myself."

"But we'd been friends for so long. Four years at university and you never even asked me out."

"You were so in demand, you were fighting for your life, fending off one unsuitable offer after another from our classmates. I wasn't going to make it worse for you."

"But you were different. You were always different."

"You said . . . let me get this right . . . you said, 'they don't see me, they see some creation of their own'."

"Well, and that was true. That's why I turned them down. God, it hurt so much, losing friendship after friendship." I was transported back to that complicated time, felt the old confusion again.

"So I didn't want to be one of them. I thought it was better to be friends than nothing. Until I saw you with him."

I put my hand to my mouth and realised it was shaking. At some deep level, this wasn't news, I'd always known it, but I'd got so used to blocking Lance from my thoughts, and here was another way for the pain to get in. "I can't do this. Not now. Please just drive."

There was a pause. Simon glanced back at me, watching me out of the corners of his eyes. I put my hand on his shoulder and he nodded, like he'd made a decision, and pulled back onto the road.

At work that night I was preoccupied, making Donna and Nora more curious.

"Who is that guy, he's . . . interesting . . . very together."

"Gravitas," said Nora, "that's what he's got."

"He's got what?"

"Like the Roman senators – dignity, presence."

"He's twenty-four!"

"Come on, tell us, who is he?"

Carl hissed through the serving hatch. "Is it local hunger day? Get that food out there."

I picked up two orders and turned towards the tables. "Come on, back to work, girls."

Donna and Nora spoke together. "Julia!" "Why aren't you telling?"

Simon finished his dinner and they sent me off early. "Go, talk, whatever. We can't watch him watching you any more."

We strolled along the river. I asked Simon questions and he talked, a smooth, rolling lull of words.

"I finished at Cambridge, graduated just after I saw you in Bruges. There were good offers, lots of interesting jobs. I took one with a big software company, easy work, and then into project management, like I said. It's, well, effortless, once you get the big picture, see how to motivate people, understand where the problems might be and pre-empt them. It's weird, I think of it as like floating above a city, looking down and understanding how the traffic flows in a way you can't when you are on the ground, in it. Now that first project is finished I'm onto the next. And now, like I said, I want to see if we can do it here."

"But you still might go back?"

"Maybe, but I think I can set up a team here. The degree course means there are lots of good programmers around and, of course, they're cheaper than in England."

"When will you know?"

"I think things will be clearer in a few weeks."

"You're not just talking about work, are you?"

He looked at me for a moment. I was relieved to see a grin. "No."

It seemed to take him all the effort he had left to open the boot to get his luggage. I took the small leather bag and led the way up the path.

"Help yourself to a shower. I'll make some tea."

"No, thanks. I'm fading, jetlagged, I guess."

"Okay, shower, then bed. Towels are in the bathroom."

I sat at the kitchen table listening to the water flow, feeling a deep longing in my chest. I trusted Simon so completely.

I took his hand as he came out, to lead him to the bedroom, but I felt a pull on my arm as he didn't follow. I turned back, stepped up and kissed him on the cheek. "I don't know what I'm doing, but I need this. Okay?"

He stared for a second then his eyes closed and he took a shallow breath. "Okay."

I lay in his arms, holding tight, and then I was sobbing, my whole body held tense and slipping out of my grip. I twisted, pulling my head down to my chest. Simon tried to pull me straight but I burrowed deeper. He wrapped around me.

"I miss him so much." My voice hiccoughed and shook. "I just don't know what to do with it. I miss the way he'd out of the blue bring me tea when I was reading, how sometimes at a party he'd ignore everyone and talk just to me. I miss the way he could be totally focused, when he was putting on his tennis gear, thinking about the game, and not even hear me speak. Just everything. Everything. Good and bad, right or wrong. It all added up to him. It's like a dead space. I want to be rid of it but at the same time I can't let it go."

My face came up and I felt Simon's cheek wet against mine. I pulled my arms around his neck, chest to chest. "And I so miss his body, the intensity of it, coming back to myself after making love and not knowing where I had been." My arms flexed around him. "I have felt so empty for so long."

Simon ran a hand along my side, from arm to hip, I felt the electric weight of it as it didn't quite settle.

"I know it's not fair, but I need to feel something. Please?" My breath held. No response. "Please. I know it's not the way you'd want it."

There was the tiniest twitch of his shoulder under my arm. "You must know I'd take you on any terms."

"Then please."

16

Donna helped me lift a chest of drawers onto spread-out newspaper.

"So tell me again what this thing is going to look like. Because it looks very ugly from here."

I smiled. "Just wait. It will be perfect, just melt into the total effect. At the moment it's ugly because it stands out; the trick is to accentuate the positive and minimise the negative – hey! you're a master of make-up, you get that."

"Yeah? I guess so."

I rubbed over the surfaces with sandpaper, then levered the lid off a tin of primer.

Donna sat on the floor, leaning against the wall. She tipped her head back and closed her eyes, stretching a leg out. I noticed her wince. As her hair fell back I saw a thumb-shaped bruise on the side of her neck. "You okay?"

Donna started. "Fine, Julia, I don't need a mother."

I walked over and pushed her hair back again. "For fuck's sake, Donna, what is that?"

She pushed my hand away angrily, almost hitting me. "Back off!"

I crouched and our faces were close together, eyes sparking. "Donna ..."

"Forget it, it's handled."

A few tense moments later I walked back and picked up my brush. There was silence as I painted one tall side of the dresser.

Donna whistled a few notes, then darted her eyes at me. "Hey, now you have to tell me, who is the guy who came into the café the other day and hasn't left since? You said he's staying here?"

"Simon. He's an old friend."

Donna grinned. "I think there may be a little more to it than that. You've been oddly secretive, and the way he watches you says sex, sex, sex."

My hand stopped in the air between brush strokes. Seconds passed, then I put the brush down and rubbed my hand across my eyebrow. "Oh, God! I don't know what to do."

"You? You always know what to do." Donna's voice was mocking, slightly unkind.

"I like him, but the timing's not right."

"How so?"

"Oh . . ." I had got so in the habit of not speaking about Lance that it was natural to avoid him again. "There's someone I haven't quite got over." I picked up the brush and continued painting.

"You had that thing with Mark."

"Yeah, but that was never serious. Simon and I have been close, as friends, for a long time. It's safer to keep it that way."

"Well, it's none of my business, but maybe you should take a reality check with him because he looks pretty far gone. I don't think he's going to take 'no' gracefully."

I lifted my brush from its smooth back and forth motion. "Really?"

"This is news to you? God, you honestly don't know what you've got, do you? You certainly don't know how to use it."

I rolled my eyes. "Of course I do. But Simon's . . . different."

"Well, if he's different, what are you waiting for?"

Maybe Donna was right. Simon was lovely, kind, always listened. It was such a relief to relax into his company. I had been protecting myself for a long time.

That night, depressed and tired after another argument with Hunter about money, I looked up into his eyes and something changed. It would feel so good to be in love again. This wasn't like I had felt about Lance – there was an ache in it, grief over affection, gratitude over grief, but the solid, comforting body became vivid and compelling.

He felt the difference in me, pulling back from my kiss and looking seriously into my eyes. "Shall I stay then? I had been thinking I should go."

"No, don't go. Stay."

17

The last apartment came on quickly, following easily on the same theme as the others. Richard, the painter, talked about the outside of the house. It was brick faced and tiled but the window surrounds needed painting. The garden was wild but he said it wouldn't take much to tidy, and some of the paths, broken concrete slabs, needed to be replaced. "I'll send my wife around, she'll tell you about the garden, she loves that sort of thing. And why not just put down stone chips instead of those slabs, you could do it in an afternoon. I'll do you an estimate for the windows and see if you can convince that landlord about it - it'll cost more if it's left, tell him that."

I talked to Hunter and he agreed uncharacteristically quickly. A cheque I had almost given up expecting lay between us. We were having coffee in my new kitchen, looking into the garden he hadn't noticed had been pruned and tidied. French windows opened onto a brick patio I had cleared and scrubbed and a bumblebee lumbered in and out again, the scent of flowers following it.

"So you agree?"

"Yes," he repeated, absently. "Look, Jules, how much longer do you think?"

I recognised his tone of voice. He wanted to hear a short time. "A couple of weeks if I work like mad. Why? I wasn't planning to move out, you know, not unless . . ."

"What?"

"Unless we move onto something else."

This had been my planned next step for a long time, but I hadn't mentioned it because Hunter was always better without too many options or too much time to think. He surprised me, however. "Exactly. That's exactly what I was going to say. We could do the same again. Of course, you wouldn't have to pay rent, in exchange for your work. You really have done a good job."

"Okay, Hunter, after that shameless flattery, what do you want?"

He looked at me winningly, hopefully. "I brought a bottle of champagne, so we could celebrate a deal."

I was suspicious. "All right, let's celebrate the principle, if not exactly the deal. And I've got an idea about this place that I think will interest you." It made sense for him to sell these apartments, make them legally separate entities and sell them individually. It wouldn't make me any money, but Hunter would gain a lot.

But he could never concentrate on business for long, unless he was counting money, and his interest was gone. The cork was out of the bottle – not champagne – and the glasses poured. "I don't suppose you're feeling sympathetic?" he asked hopefully. "Cyndy has been so moody again."

"Any reason?" I asked, idly.

His face clouded over and he hesitated. "Well, she found out something." Fizzy wine slopped onto the table. He pulled a mangled tissue from his pocket and for a few moments appeared absorbed in wiping it up.

"But, I mean, a man needs comfort."

I sighed, wondering about this relationship I only saw half of. Then an idea occurred. Perhaps Hunter would be more malleable with Cyndy around. I sat up straight. "You know I'd love to meet her. Do you think she'd invite me to lunch?"

Hunter's hand clenched on the tissue. "Oh, no, I don't think . . . I don't think she'd be very happy if she met you, she'd think . . ." Never clever enough to stop himself in time.

I looked him directly, but not unkindly, in the eye. "I'm sure I'd have no trouble convincing her I will never be a threat."

Hunter gazed at me sadly. "Never?"

"That's right. Never."

18

Hunter acted without consulting me and I stood looking at the block of flats he had bought in dismay. It was awful: square, cramped and in a marginal part of town.

"Let me guess," I felt my right hand form an involuntary fist. "It was cheap."

"A bargain." Hunter nodded proudly. "What do you think?"

"I think we've got a lot to talk about. But I can't do it here."

There was an awkward pause until Hunter realised he should pay for the coffees, then I led him to a table and sat down.

"Right, I'll be blunt. They are awful." His face fell. "But that doesn't mean we can't do something. A quick turnover is all they're worth, some paint, a brush up of kitchens and bathrooms, but no more; and in the meantime, I'll look around for something better, with real potential where we can add a lot of value. But here's the deal. Free rent isn't enough any more. If you want me in, then I want a cut of the gain, half the profit. We take the selling cost, subtract the buy price and the costs and split the rest."

Hunter was bamboozled. "I don't understand."

I took him through it slowly. "You bought it. We do it up. We sell it.

Hopefully the sale price is higher than the buy price and the costs. That's the profit. I take half."

"Half my money?"

"In exchange for all the work." Not to mention all the talent. "If I don't do it, there is no profit."

There was a long pause. Slowly Hunter realised this was true, but parting with half . . . "A third."

I sighed, but at least it was something. It was enough. "Okay. Deal." I reached out to shake Hunter's hand and forced a smile to keep things friendly. "I'll have my lawyers draw up a contract," I said, in a mock American accent.

The original flats were sold and Simon had bought an apartment in the centre of town. I refused to live in the flats Hunter had bought so I moved in with Simon.

"But I'll pay you rent."

"Come on, you didn't charge me."

"I know it doesn't make sense, it's just that I've had this glimpse of achieving something on my own. I want to pay my own way."

"This place is an investment, it will pay for itself in the end. Look, you provide the furniture, then we'll be square, if that's what you really want."

He was nice about it but my painted wood and loose covered sofas didn't look right against the modern architecture. I continued to worry about this in the background, but it was soon overtaken by the reality of the renovation.

I came back from a dispiriting day, too tired to wash the paint out of my hair. I fell onto the sofa, letting my hand fall to the floor and woke when Simon came in half an hour later. He leaned over to kiss me. "Tough day?"

I turned my head and looked up at him.

"Shall I take you out for dinner? You look a little low."

"I can't be bothered to change. There's some soup in the cupboard. Then would you read to me? Some poetry? I've spent all day in that horrible hole, in the dark and the cold, and I want to imagine some beauty."

"How is it going?"

"Slow. It seems very slow, there's no flow when my heart isn't in it. I just want to forget it for tonight."

We ate in silence. I felt Simon's eyes on me.

"What?"

"Something's different."

I shrugged. "It's just this project."

"No. It's more. I've been trying to figure it out. I knew you were unhappy, but under the surface you were still you. Now it's like something has gone, like you've given up on something."

"I don't know. I'm too tired to think about it."

"You used to keep a journal."

"Yeah. But I got tired of writing the same thing over and over and getting nowhere."

"Can't you work it through?"

"No. I tried, but it just hurts too much. Something positive to work on gave me hope, but now with these awful flats, I've got nothing. Except you." My mouth twitched. I bit the inside of my lower lip to keep it still.

Simon came around the table and knelt beside me, pulling me round to look down into his face. "Baby, I so want you to get better. I'd give anything to have you real and alive again."

I nodded but I couldn't speak for a minute. "I don't want to feel like this. I'm doing everything I can to snap out of it. But it's not going to happen tonight. So just read to me, please?"

I brought him T.S. Eliot. He has a gorgeous voice, mid-pitch and fluid, and he can take it far away, like magic, into another world. "Prufrock?"

Simon sat on the sofa and I perched on the edge of the coffee table opposite. He watched me for a moment. "Julia . . ."

"Just read."

He began on "The Love Song of J. Alfred Prufrock". I listened, and as he forgot me and lost himself in the words I fixed my eyes on his face, as if I could read his soul there. He looked up when he had finished.

"Read it again." As he began I moved to sit on the floor, head against his leg. I felt him close the book, reciting from memory. He pulled my hair across his knee and his hand moved in a slow rhythm along its length. The peace flowing from his hand was such a relief, I could have sat that way forever.

19

Simon had his team together and the project was underway. He turned up at the flats one evening, excited.

"Julia?" He knocked on the open door. I was crouched on the floor painting a skirting. "How's it going?"

"It's too cold, the paint won't go on properly. I spent the day washing down the outside, getting ready to do that as soon as we get a fine day, but when it got dark I thought I'd try again in here. I feel like I haven't been warm for centuries."

He took the brush out of my hand. "Come on, I've got good news. Come out and celebrate with me."

"But . . ." I sighed. "Okay. I'll lock up. Wrap that brush for me, would you?"

In the restaurant I began to thaw out. A waitress carried a stack of plates out of the kitchen. I had taken a few weeks off work and felt nostalgic watching her.

"I'd forgotten what normal life is. I feel like I haven't seen anyone for ages. Hey, let's get together with Donna and Nora this weekend. Eddy, too, I guess."

Simon groaned. "Oh! Not Eddy, he's as witty as a breadfruit. And he's a snake – brutal behind those hooded eyes."

"You're exaggerating. He's not so bad."

"It's fine for you, you go off, the three of you, like some teenage girls' club. Can't Nora find a boyfriend? She'd probably have better taste."

"Donna's a sweetheart underneath."

"She's fucked up – self-destruct on auto-pilot."

"It's not that bad!" My voice was loud and people turned. "You don't know her."

"Every time we see her there's a new bruise and a new excuse."

I blew out a breath. "I know. But I don't know what to do about it."

"Look, get together with the girls, Eddy, too, if you want, but count me out. Now, can we change the subject? I want to tell you my news. We made an advance sale today, which means I get my completion bonus early. Let's take a trip, my treat. Somewhere amazing, outback Australia – we could take one of those trans-continental trains."

"Simon . . ."

"I know. You can't take time off, you're broke and you don't want me to pay. Well get over it. Let Hunter wait. I want this, and I'm not going on my own."

As the desert rolled by my frustration fell away and my soul opened out into the wide space. I had thought I would read but I found myself staring endlessly, time punctuated by night and day, the movement of the passing landscape, the promptings of my stomach. As the train rolled out of Alice on the second day, the sun setting against the huge blue sky and the reflection of my gold-flooded face playing tricks with the view, a question rose from deep within me.

"Do you want children, Simon?"

He looked up from his book. I watched his reflection watching mine. "Yes, some day."

"So do I." I thought dreamily of what a great father he would make, seeing images of a laughing curly-headed child swinging in his arms. "It seems like a good time, now."

His shadow face frowned, as if he had a question, but it was a long time before he spoke. "You're talking about my child?"

"Yes."

"Look at me."

I turned my face towards the real him, my eyes settling on the air in front of his eyes. "No, at me! You're not here with me, and I can't have this conversation this way, wake up!"

I felt myself pulled from somewhere and his face became solid. It was an effort and I resisted.

"I want to hear you say that this baby will be mine, too. Mine."

"Of course." I leaned forward across the table between us and put a hand on his cheek. "Of course."

His eyes flicked back and forth between mine. "God, you're exasperating! You flit in and out of your body like a ghost. It drives me crazy never knowing whether you'll be there or not." He took my hand between his. I didn't want to acknowledge what he was saying so I sat still.

"Well, shall we?"

His head tilted and his eyes moved from mine, imagining. "Yeah, I'd like it."

I smiled, following his gaze back to the window to where the sun had disappeared, a half-circle glow remaining. I drifted back into my dream again.

20

Life was back to normal. I hadn't realised how hard I'd been to live with until the renovation was over and I was free. I never wanted to set foot there again. Now they were all but sold and I couldn't wait to have some money and start on something new, with soul this time.

I watched Simon in the kitchen. It was my night off from the café and he had come home early to cook. The phone rang and he wiped his hands to answer it. I sipped my wine, concentrating on the Vogue-pose I was practising, feet up on the coffee table and both hands around my glass.

"It's Hunter."

I looked at my watch. "The sale on the last unit was being finalised today. Maybe he just wants to tell me it's all done."

I listened quietly as Hunter told me the bad news. There had been a last minute hitch, the buyer had tried to pull out and Hunter had accepted a lower price to close the sale.

"How could that happen? The contracts were finalised weeks ago."

The drone of his voice made some sort of sense, fumbling legalese but plausible, but then he continued. He'd been doing the sums, it wasn't as good as we thought. Blah, blah, blah. But then the final point hit home and I understood what he was saying.

"Nothing! What the hell do you mean?"

The conversation disintegrated from there. I don't even know what I said, but finally I flicked off the phone, barely restraining myself from throwing it across the room.

"Shit! Shit, shit, shit!"

"What is it?"

"Shit, Simon, it's nothing, ignore me, I'll be okay in a few minutes, I'll figure it out."

But I couldn't. Simon put dinner on the table and I ate in preoccupied silence, then jumped up to clear immediately. Simon, darling angel, waited.

I set the dishwasher going, but the kitchen annoyed me and I began emptying out cupboards, sorting things, wiping them and putting them away again. Simon sat reading, looking up every now and then. At ten o'clock, still hyped, I grabbed my key. "I think I'll just go for a walk."

"It's quite late."

"I know."

"Want me to come?"

"No, I just need to walk off some steam, I won't be long."

Next morning I was still rattled. Simon put toast down on the table in front of me as I drank strong black coffee.

"Okay, enough. What's going on?"

I looked up at him and sighed. "Okay. Figuring it out myself isn't working, so . . . It's Hunter, the shit! He's playing the fool with the profit from the flats. I agreed to a third, even though I did all the work. But now he says he's charging interest on the money he invested, as expense before the split, even though that was all he put into the deal. The little cretin says

I owe him money. Shit! Little shit! Even though I have the contract, the sale price goes through him, and he's supposed to pay me. Greedy little bastard. He says 'sue him' but of course, he knows that would cost more than he owes me."

Simon was still for a moment. "Do you think he really means it?"

I threw myself back in my chair, took a deep breath through my nose and held it for a second. "No," I said. "No, he probably just wants to cut what he pays me." I closed my eyes and put my hand across my mouth, squeezing my nose, then put my hand up at shoulder level in a fist. I exhaled fast. "I just need to get a grip, work out what to do. Ungrateful bastard. Lazy ungrateful sod. We were all set to move on to the next one, and this was going to be fun, something special, like the first. But I'm not going in with him again, and certainly not for nothing. That's what he suggested, that I pay him off by doing the next one. Shit! Shit! Shit! Little shit!"

"When does he get the money?"

"Yesterday, he'll have it now. Damn, I'm supposed to be at work at ten, I need to figure out what I'm going to do and I need to sort this out."

"Phone Carl, he'll understand. And you know Hunter's really scared of you, he's a lightweight. The only way he'll win is if you lose your temper. So get calm, go down there and stand in front of him until he gives you a cheque."

I thought about the scene Simon had just painted and gave a short laugh. "You're right. He can hide behind the threat of lawyers, he can bluster, and he caught me off guard yesterday. But he always caves in if I look him in the eye for long enough." I took a deep breath and began to create a mental picture of myself coming out of his office with a cheque and a smile.

"Hey, drop me down there? Just give me five minutes to get dressed."

21

As I stood outside Hunter's office door I felt a slight buzz. I hated confrontation, didn't I? But somehow I was looking forward to this, spoiling for a fight. There had been months of petty hassles, financial denial, small events not worth getting worked up over, buried and swallowed. Now was my time. I'd make the little bastard squirm. I took a breath, realising I needed to focus on the outcome. What did I want? A cheque? No, I wanted to watch him transfer the money on the Internet, no possibility for reneging. Part of me wanted to humiliate him, but even as I recognised that I felt myself draw up with a slow inward breath. I closed my eyes. I just wanted the money, so I could move on with the things I wanted to do.

As I put my hand on the door I glanced along the hall. The morning sun shone through a tulip window, bouncing red light off the wall. Something shifted outside, perhaps a cloud moving, and as I watched, the glow intensified. I pushed forward without knocking and walked inside.

"Hey Hunter. I've come to work things out."

He crouched down in his chair. I saw he had been expecting me, the hunter had become the hunted.

"Julia, now listen . . ."

"No, you listen. There's a simple way to get me out of here with no blood shed. $24,500."

"Julia . . ."

"Hunter, how else do you think we are going to resolve this? It's less than expected. For whatever reason you took less . . ."

He bowed over suddenly and put his hands over his head. The effect was like a protester lying down in front of a bulldozer. "Okay, what is it?"

"Cyndy's left me. And I'm sick."

I stared at his bald spot, wondering what I felt. Exasperated. "And this affects me because?"

He looked up and I saw he was crying.

"Sick how?"

He looked away again. Probably an STI from whatever mindless bint he could persuade to sleep with him.

"I can't pay you because Cyndy needs to sign."

"I don't believe you."

"It's true." Uncharacteristically brief for him, no slippery wordiness.

Damn. What now? No point wishing things were different. Pure anger rose up behind my eyes and I felt powerful. He looked back and my eyes locked his. His head tilted down but he held my gaze.

"Start talking."

And it came out. He'd been bankrupt, all flash and no substance. Cyndy had salvaged their house and a couple of other assets and built things up again, but kept him on a short leash. The house where I first met him was hers. The project we had been working on was hers. While he slunk about town looking cool in his red BMW, she owned everything. But as long as he got to look good, he didn't really care. As he spoke, he gradually straightened in his chair. I had a fleeting impression of myself as priest hearing his confession.

"And the deal you made with me?"

"She didn't know about it."

Well, there was a way forward. I could talk to her. But that added complication and I wanted out, quick and simple. I ran my eyes around the room looking for inspiration. There was a way of getting this resolved now, I could feel it. My search stopped at a photograph on the desk, Hunter lounging across the bonnet of his car.

"The BMW, is it yours or Cyndy's?"

He went pale.

"Okay, come on. We'll do a swap."

On his face, close behind horror at his penance came hope of absolution.

I threw the car keys on the table in front of Simon that night. He looked up, questioning and I told him the story. The image of Hunter behind the wheel of my old Corolla made me laugh; I felt deliciously cruel and cold-hearted.

"I was going to sell the BMW right away, as soon as the change of ownership came through. I went to a dealer and they gave me a price. But then I thought, I don't really need the money until I find a place to buy. And I kind of like the feel of driving it."

Simon raised his eyebrows.

"I know. Weird, huh? But I'm going with it."

I had stopped at a bakery on the way home and bought a doughnut, an old weakness I rarely gave in to. Simon went back to his magazine and I took it out, smoothing the brown paper bag to place it on.

"Dinner?" he asked, glancing up.

"I felt like celebrating."

Unusually unselfconscious I focused all my senses on the bun, feeling the rasp and zing of the sugar, the oil of the dough. I felt every grain that stuck to my lips, pushing further out onto my face as I pursued it, licking in circles. The texture of the cream was smooth, with no taste to distract as it slid across the surface of my tongue. When I looked up Simon was watching, fascinated.

"Hedonist."

I grinned. "Yeah, I know."

He reached across and wiped a spot of cream from the corner of my mouth with his thumb and licked it off. "Okay, that's dinner for me. Time for bed."

"Shall we go out after work?" Donna suggested.

"Sure, I'll text Nora." Nora had finished her degree and left the café once she had got her government department job.

"What's happening with Donna?" Nora asked, when she came in at closing time. "Eddy usually wants her home straight away."

I shrugged. Donna was in high spirits and we just followed along. She chose a noisy bar where it was difficult to talk, leaning forward and shouting to be heard.

"Eddy's gone."

"What! What happened?"

Her eyes were bright, with excitement or tears I couldn't tell. "He hit me - well, it's not the first time - so I kicked him out."

Nora and I stared at each other. She had never admitted it before. I reached out and put a hand on her shoulder.

"Are you okay?" I shouted.

"Yeah, I guess. There's just one thing . . . I'm pregnant."

This was ridiculous - we couldn't have this conversation here. I grabbed them both by an arm and pulled them outside, hailing a taxi. But really there wasn't much else to say. Eddy didn't know about the baby, and among other parting shots had said he was happy to go, so Donna didn't fear him coming back.

"What about the baby - are you happy?" It should have been me. What was I waiting for? Envy snaked upwards and for a moment I hated her. Could she feel it?

She looked directly at me, orange light from street lamps regularly scanning her face through the taxi window. "I don't know. It doesn't feel real yet. I don't feel very much either way."

22

Donna was behind in her rent and it was easier to let the flat go than try to catch up.

"I wish I could help her . . . do you think we could have her to stay for a while, until she gets on her feet?"

Simon turned in his chair. "I'd rather give her money."

"You know she wouldn't take it. I know you don't have much in common, but she has nowhere else to go."

He shook his head. "Okay, sure, whatever." He came over to where I was arranging pictures on the table. "What are you doing?"

"I've got an idea for a business. I want to have something of my own set up before we have a baby, and I've been thinking about this for a while. People like my furniture, I think I can sell it – things like the dressers and cupboards and chests of drawers. I'm putting together an album, but also I need some more pieces, to show what I can do. What do you think? I want something I can do from home."

"Sounds like a good idea. You can start slow, see how it goes."

"Exactly! And keep working in the café in the meantime."

I had planned to buy a house to renovate but that would wait. Things were good between Simon and me and I was enjoying spending time in a place that was finished.

Donna watched me sanding, at a loose end until she had to go to work. She stepped back as I opened a tin of paint. "Oh, I feel sick. Do you have some bread or something to settle my stomach?"

"Sure. In the kitchen. Open the window, too, if you want." She looked awful, moving slowly around the house with occasional dashes to the bathroom. "How long will the sickness last?"

Donna shrugged. "They said till twelve weeks, and I'm twenty, so who knows? Just one of the many ways Nature favours her chosen ones."

"But how do you work, if you feel like this?"

"Grim determination, I guess. I keep having Technicolor visions of hurling over a load of meals. Seriously, where would I find another job now?"

I glanced up as I continued to paint. Donna was leaning back against the table. Her eyes were closed and her hand was on her stomach.

"What are you going to do once the baby comes?"

"The million dollar question."

I waited, but she said nothing else. After a while she looked up.

"So you're going to sell this weird stuff? Who to?"

Of all the questions I had about the business, this was the easiest one to answer. I knew every furniture shop in town, from exploring to find what I needed, and the more expensive ones because it was entertaining to look, to see what was available, understand current fashion and think about how the shops had arranged things. Still I thought about it over and over again. What would I say? Just the thought of going in and asking was terrifying.

Three weeks later I knew I had enough to start selling. I was still hesitating, but after a while I realised that not doing it was probably worse than doing it. Inaction was like paralysis.

It was time to get a portfolio together.

I picked up the phone. "Hey, Nora, I need a hand. Have you got half an hour? And can you bring your digital camera?"

We moved the pieces around so the light was good and I photographed each one from several angles.

"So tell me again why we are doing this?"

"I need another way of making a living, apart from the café."

"So you're going to sell your furniture? This doesn't strike me as a long-term plan."

"No, well, yes, I suppose I would. But these are to show the buyers at the shops, get orders. I'll do more."

Nora tilted her head. "This is just one of the differences between you and me. I would never think to do this, and if I did, I would have no idea where to start. What will you say?"

I shrugged and spoke with false confidence. "I know this stuff will sell. I've seen things like it in magazines. So I'll just show them the pictures and ask if they're interested."

"Just like that?"

"Sure, why not? It's information. They'll want to know." It was bizarre, real confidence was building as I talked. "And maybe I'll just hint at the other places I'm talking to – there must be a lot of competition between the bigger shops, they don't want the others to have something they haven't. So we'll see . . . You know I'm just making this up as I go along, right? What is there to lose?" I opened a cupboard slightly and took a last shot.

"You know, you are just amazing."

I looked over my shoulder. "Why would you say that? This is all obvious, it's just because I've haunted the shops and thought about it. It's only about seeing what's in front of me."

We downloaded the photographs on Simon's computer and I chose the best ones. I looked back through my apartment shots and found a few good ones there, then sent them through to a local camera shop via their website to print.

Nora sat back in the second office chair. "I wish I had your imagination. And courage." She sounded low.

"How is work?'

"Dull, like you said it would be. I could handle that, but everyone's so negative, complaining about the boss, complaining about the hours."

"Will you look for something else?"

"With a degree in English literature what else can I do?"

"Lots of things! Lots. Are you writing?"

"A little. A short story or two. But the malaise has got in there, too."

"Well, why not come back to the café, part time? At least the staff are friendly. We'd keep your spirits up."

"I don't know. By the time I get home I'm shattered."

"You're okay today."

"It's Saturday. Have a look at me tomorrow, about 5 o'clock. That's when I start the mental downward slide to Monday."

"You can't stay there. Just resign. There are other jobs out there."

"Well, get this business off the ground and I'll come and work for you."

I grinned. "It's a deal."

23

I stood outside a small antique shop with my heart beating hard. Gotta do it; just do it. Now, while the shop is empty. My arm was weak and I had to fall against the door to get it to open.

"Hi." My voice cracked.

"Hello."

I had met the woman many times and she turned back to her desk, expecting me to browse. I waited till she turned back.

"Can I help you?"

"Yes. I was wondering, I have a line of furniture I have been working on, and I think it would complement what you have here . . . I have photographs."

The woman straightened, posture sharper, resistant. There was a momentary pause. I stepped over with the folder and opened it so that it was easier for her to look at it than not. After a few pages she relaxed slightly and nodded at one or two.

"We mainly sell antiques . . ."

"But not only."

"Perhaps." She continued looking through. "This one is pretty . . . And what a good idea, the kitchen sink!"

"Could I bring something in, and you could see if it sells?"

"Well, it's not only my decision. Philippa, who owns the shop, is not here this morning." She spoke reluctantly. I had never before had the impression she was not the owner herself. "Why don't you leave these and I'll show them to her."

"I'm sorry, this is the only copy I have. It's a boutique business, an exclusive line, which is why I thought of here. Do you know when she'll be in? Perhaps I should come back."

"She usually comes in to close up."

"5:30?"

"Around then."

"She must have a lot of faith in you, to trust you with her business." Was I shameless? Where did this transparent flattery come from?

The woman seemed to swallow it, though. "Yes, I think she does."

"Well, thanks for taking time with me. I appreciate your input, with your knowledge of furniture, it's valuable."

The woman sat up proudly. "I'll tell Philippa about it, and say you are coming back."

I had planned to go into another shop or two along the street, but I needed to regroup. Nora's words drifted through my head. "I wouldn't have a clue where to start, what to say."

My whole being screamed at me to go home, give up, but I had to come back at closing time anyway. I went into a café, ordered a hot chocolate, picked up a magazine. Ten minutes later I took another deep breath. If I didn't keep going, that would be the end of my business.

The next shop was a straight "no". And the next. The fourth was more promising: "Interesting, but not quite our style. Have you tried Brown Antiques?"

"Yes."

"Delilah?"

"In High Street?"

"Yes."

"No, I haven't. Thanks."

I had been planning to stop after this one, but I drove to Delilah feeling optimistic. This time there was a small success: a minimal nod from the owner as she looked at the pictures. "Bring in a pair of these bedside cabinets, and we'll see what the reaction is."

I contained my elation until I was in the car, then threw my hands up in a gesture of victory. "Yes! I am on my way!"

24

It was slow, but it was happening. I lived on my wages from the café and spent my spare hours building up stock. Two shops took a couple of pieces each, and when those sold, they took more. Martin, at Windermere Furniture, began with three bigger pieces in the window, and this produced a lot of interest and a few orders. I talked to him about the difficulty of finding enough good second-hand pieces to use.

Martin leaned his solid bulk back against his desk. He knew I was coming in and I had a feeling he had dressed up – combed his usually ruffled hair into a less unruly frizz, put on a tidy jumper. He moved the cream bun on the desk out of sight behind him. He needn't have bothered.

"Long term, a more consistent line of stock would be better anyway. What about approaching one of the local furniture makers and doing a wholesale deal? You could have some input into the designs, simplify them a little so they are cheaper to make, get them made up in pine, or even something cheaper, since you're going to paint them. They'll be a little more expensive than the old pieces, but more reliable and you won't have to spend time looking for them."

"Yes, I see . . . but I wouldn't have any idea where to start." I looked at the floor for a moment then looked up at Martin and grinned. "But I bet you would."

He grinned back. "Sure. I'll make a few calls, Christchurch is a small town, we tend to know each other – although never let on that I've been talking to anyone at the lower end of the market. I'll have a chat to one or two importers as well, they may be able to bring in some stock unfinished, although there will be a long order time."

"Thanks, that would be great!"

"Hey, I heard someone say when you were in the other day that you're working at Carl's Café as a waitress."

"Yeah, sure – this doesn't quite pay the rent yet."

"Interesting. I'm surprised. If you ever need a business partner, give me a call. We could take this stuff national."

"I'll keep it in mind." I turned to go.

"So tell me about the café, what's it like?"

"I love it, the energy of the people, the friends I work with, and it's good exercise. And it fits really well with this, the perfect contrast."

I watched Martin's reaction. Something in his face told me he was about to make a move towards asking me out. I switched the conversation back to him.

"Tell me about your business, Martin. How long have you been in it?"

"My family has always worked with furniture – I grew up polishing things and making small repairs for Dad's shop. You just sort of absorb it, and I'm not qualified to do anything else. I couldn't work for someone else, anyway. So I potter along here. Things are changing, though, furniture is far more about fashion than it used to be."

"Yes?"

He laughed. "In fact, I can usually tell by the hairstyle of a woman what sort of furniture she will want. I can even picture the rooms it will go in, after fifteen years of delivering, first with my parents and now here. The psychology of it is part of what keeps it interesting."

"Married, Martin?"

He tilted his head to the side and back, and flicked his eyebrows up. "I was. She left. No kids, thank goodness . . . I'd have loved them, but I couldn't have stood having them taken away. I have a weakness for beautiful things, but that's not the best basis for a relationship." He looked at me out of the corner of his eye. "You?"

There was a pause. "Simon keeps asking."

Martin's eyes sharpened into a more intelligent expression. "So there's hope for me yet?"

I kept my voice light. "I don't see myself settling down – freedom is such a big thing; and somewhere, to be uncovered, I have dreams that require me to be independent, do it all on my own." I found I was talking more to myself. "Actually, I don't know what the hell I'm doing, but the mention of marriage sends me into a panic."

"Well, maybe I'll drop by the café, say hi."

"I'd like that. And if you want me to set you up with someone, just say the word."

His answer was a joke and not a joke. "So what are we waiting for?"

I looked into his kind eyes. This guy was made for marriage, to the right woman. He deserved to be adored. "Actually, there is someone . . . she'd be almost good enough for you."

He grinned sheepishly. "I'm nothing special."

"Don't kid yourself, Babe, you're the catch of the year."

Simon edged around painting materials and scattered pieces of a chest of drawers to bring pasta to the table. Nora had come over to help me paint and he was cooking for both of us.

"Sorry, guys," I picked up a pile of mail from the other end of the table and dumped it on the floor. "I guess things are getting away on me a little."

Simon was unperturbed. "Just our Julia, always different and always the same."

"I know you're going crazy with a mess in every room, but I'll get this order out by Friday and we'll be back to normal."

Nora leaned forward to take the bowl from Simon. "Donna moved out?"

I glanced at him and cut in before he could speak. "Yeah, last weekend. Hey, Nora, what did you think of Martin?"

Nora shook her head. "No, Julia."

"You went to his shop like I told you. Did you talk to him?"

"He said 'hello', I said 'hello'."

"No more?"

"The shop was crowded. So, no, that was it. What did you expect?"

"A little more effort. He could be perfect for you!"

"Julia! He's fat and old."

"Nora, I'm surprised at you! He's a nice guy who adores children and has his own business. What's up? You know I wouldn't set you up with someone who wasn't worthy of you."

"Worthy of me? You make me sound like a princess." She laughed.

"Well, you are, to me. You deserve the best."

"He's just not what I pictured for my handsome prince . . . Oh, don't look at me like that! All right. But if I have a terrible time, I'm blaming you." She turned in her chair. "Simon, how do you put up with this sort of thing?"

"She hasn't tried to match-make for me for a long time, thank goodness."

Nora laughed. "I didn't mean that, I meant . . . Oh, pass the parmesan. You can give him my number. If he wants, he can give me a call."

25

I felt Simon watch as I covered a fourth piece of toast with butter and jam.

"J, is there any chance you might be pregnant?"

I felt my secret joy bubble up inside me. "Yeah, I just might be."

An uncertain laugh escaped him. "Wow."

"I didn't know how I'd feel, but I just feel fantastic – can't you see me, like one of those Leonardo Madonnas, all serene and content?"

"That's a pretty surreal image."

"Well, are you pleased?"

"Of course. I'm just absorbing it . . ."

"You're wondering what will happen now, with us."

He shrugged.

"Can't things just stay as they are? There's so much happening, with work, and the furniture and everything."

"I've always wanted this, the home, the family. But there was a wife in the picture as well."

"I know, I just . . ."

"I'm not going to push it, but if you'd like the ring, the whole romantic thing, just let me know, I've got it all planned out."

A few weeks later I found myself getting restless. First I started moving things around in the apartment, then I stopped by a real estate office and picked up their magazine.

"What do you think about moving?"

"Why? Aren't you happy here?"

"Yeah . . . but I've been thinking I'd like to buy a place of my own. I don't know, maybe I'm nesting. You know I planned to get something to renovate sooner or later."

"It just doesn't seem like the best time. You're busy with the furniture and renovating is physical work."

"That's another thing – I need more space. You've been great about it, but it's hard, living in this chaos."

"You could get a workshop, do the furniture there."

"Once the baby comes I'll need to be working at home if I'm going to get anything done."

Simon pulled his shoulders back, took a slow breath. "You really want this?"

"Yeah, I do."

"Okay, sure, whatever. Whatever you need."

Being pregnant was like being in love, a secret future. I floated above everything for the next few months, delivering furniture, house hunting. Simon was thoughtful, cooking and looking after me. I felt peaceful and loved.

I took possession of the house when I was seven months' pregnant. At the moment I opened the door I was tired and lacking imagination. Consciously I knew it would be great when it was finished – I had had such a clear vision when I looked at it six weeks before – but now, still muddy outside and mouldy inside after a wet winter, it was depressing.

I set to work, cleaning cupboards. Washing walls would have to wait until I could climb a ladder again. I hadn't quite thought that through before.

Simon came by after work. I answered his knock and went straight back to the kitchen, then appeared in the doorway again when he didn't follow. "Julia," he said quietly, looking around at the damp room. "You can't bring the baby here."

"Simon, what do you mean? This is my home, the first I've ever owned. It will be magical."

"Maybe, but at the moment it is . . . look, why not stay at the apartment until it's fixed? I'm serious now."

"We've talked about this, I thought you understood."

"I get it, you want to build a home. I'm not stopping you doing that."

"Simon, I'm tired, and I can't think straight."

"Exactly."

"Exactly, so this is not the right time to talk about this. Can't I just be happy? This is my first house, it should be exciting." I was so disappointed I wanted to cry. I walked over to him and put my hands on his chest.

"And it will be. But at the moment it's not healthy. It's clear it will be better for the baby if we stay at the apartment, for a few months at least."

I stepped back from him. "Simon, I'm going to do this." I glared at him but he didn't back down.

"There is no room for argument, it's obvious. And beyond that, we should get married. You always change the subject when I get near it. I've been patient, but you're not even trying. Now, for the baby's sake, we need to get it sorted out."

The hairs rose on my arms and neck. I felt the baby kick, hard, with the surge of emotion, and it only made me more angry. I stood absolutely still, feeling my eyes sparking cold. "A hell of a proposal, Simon." His gaze flickered away and back. "Get out."

26

I sat quiet and still in the window seat. My head was buzzing. What had just happened? My confidence had gone but why had I taken that out on Simon? I reached into my bag for a notebook and pen.

I feel like everything is falling apart. The baby will be here soon and I'm not ready. How can I be a good mother when I can't even give us a good home? Simon's kind and funny and beautiful and I keep pushing him away. What am I scared of? He would give us everything and ask for nothing but the thought of letting him do that is scarier than anything. It doesn't make sense. I wish I could make it make sense.

Maybe I just needed to take the plunge and trust him.

Work at the café was getting harder; I was flushed and short of breath a lot of the time. Carl noticed. "Hey Babe, maybe it's time to slow down a little."

"I'm fine, don't you start."

He stepped back and raised his hands in the air. "Julia, you don't fit between the tables any more."

I was about to protest, then laughed, but my shoulders fell. "You're right. But I still need the money. A few weeks more?"

"Well, what about moving into the kitchen? We can set up a wide-woman's zone, you can do prep for me."

I thought for a moment. "Sure. Thanks."

Carl watched as I turned a glass in my hand. "Anything up?"

I shrugged. He hesitated, then pulled me into a hug. "You'll be fine, both of you."

He felt so solid and safe. I hung on for a moment. "Yeah. I know."

Nora and Donna and Donna's baby, Damien, were coming over that evening; I wanted the warmth of friends to cheer the place up. Simon lit the fire and I turned on all the lights – I had replaced the 40-watt bulbs with 100s and put lamps in every corner. It was beginning to feel like home.

Donna was desperate for any opportunity to get out of her flat; but Damien seemed easy, feeding quietly and going back to sleep – "He sleeps in the evening so he has the energy to be up all night."

The mood was still cool between Simon and me. He was sleeping here but most of his clothes were still at his apartment and it didn't feel like he had really moved in.

Over dinner there was a discussion about film stars. Nora gazed dreamily into the distance talking about Keanu Reeves. Donna's taste was more for older men: George Clooney, even, oddly, Woody Allen. Simon, when pressed, listed three women. I was surprised by my reaction. "Weird, I'm jealous."

"I didn't think you capable of jealousy. You never seemed to be jealous over Lance." His voice was cold. I looked up, straight into his eyes, furious.

He held my gaze defiantly.

Donna ignored the tension. "Lance? Who is Lance?"

I looked at the table. "Was. Lance was my husband." I was crying.

Donna, always volatile, and now short of sleep, chose to take offence. "You were married!" she thundered, "And you didn't tell us? What the fuck is our friendship about?" I saw Nora put a hand out to stop her.

"I don't want to talk about it. That's not my life any more." I felt an intense, aching sadness and tears were flooding down my cheeks. Everyone was staring.

Simon touched my shoulder but I shrugged him off, ran into the bedroom and threw myself onto the bed. I heard Nora through the open door. "But Simon, why is she so upset? She's in love with you."

"You think so? I think we've just seen she's still in love with Lance. Maybe that is what all this is about."

"All what? Did they get divorced?"

"He's dead. Perfection set in stone. Oh, bugger it. I'm sick of feeling like this." A few seconds later I heard the front door slam.

LAW OF ATTRACTION

27

I thought I loved this baby more than my life, but I found, when I thought the birth was going to kill me, that it wasn't true. Feeling my sanity slipping I begged for drugs, to stop the pain whatever the cost. Minutes later she was born, and it was over, but that moment of weakness remained with me, humbling.

I watched Simon look down at Maria, quiet in his arms. He held her carefully and focused on her face. I felt a pang of jealousy, excluded, but it melted when he handed her back, sharing the love in his eyes with me, too. My passion for her took hold of me again.

"I called your mother, she's coming this afternoon."

Mum. Did she feel like this about me when I was born? Did she still? "Thanks." I sensed Simon hesitate. "What?"

"I called Mum, too. She'd like to visit."

My stomach churned over. I hadn't seen Sheila since I left after the funeral. Whenever Simon went to visit, I made an excuse. I had no idea what he had told her, or what she thought about him and me.

"Of course. Any time."

"I'll bring her in tonight. Did they say when you can go home?"

"Tomorrow morning."

"You don't mind her coming?"

"Of course not." I shifted uncomfortably. "I'd like a shower before Mum arrives. Would you ring the bell for the nurse?"

What did I feel? Despite everything, was I still desperate for Sheila's approval? It didn't make sense, but I knew I was.

Mum came, bringing a tiny cardigan she had knitted and bath salts for me. I watched her hang lovingly over Maria, my heart full. Then Simon went to get Sheila. Maria fretted as I sat, nervously, waiting.

She greeted me quietly and took the baby in her arms. I watched her soften and saw an echo of her love for her boys. She turned to Simon and beamed. Was this the beginning of the thaw? "She's lovely, darling." Then she turned to me. "Well done, Dear."

I began to get uneasy, a primeval instinct telling me she had held Maria too long. I stretched out my arms. Sheila saw the movement and handed her to Simon, who brought her to me. She smelled of Sheila's perfume. My nose twitched.

"And can I hope for a wedding?"

I looked up at Simon. With Maria back in my arms I felt powerful. What was there to be afraid of, after all? "Perhaps."

For the first few months I kept Maria with me all the time, carrying her from room to room if she was awake, moving the bassinet to where I was working if she was sleeping, and picking her up as soon as she woke and began to call. She was bright, interested, engaging, and I loved her blindly.

Simon spent as much time as he could at home, setting up a computer in a corner of my workroom. He paced with Maria in the evenings so I could work and we fell into an easy rhythm, time dictated by feeding, changing, sleeping. For the moment I was happy not thinking beyond each day.

Donna was having a much harder time, resentful of being on her own, and in the habit of complaining that young Damien was trying to ruin her life.

"Sometimes I think it's either him or me."

I took him from his car seat and put him against my shoulder.

"Donna, he's perfect: healthy, alert . . ."

"He's the devil. Whenever I put my head on my pillow to sleep, it's like an alarm going off. I try to go out, to regain some sanity, and he needs changing, or he throws up, and by the time I get that sorted he's crying again because he's hungry. I swear, he wants to keep me prisoner. God, he's got some of his dad in him – that's right, smile at Aunty Julia, make me a liar."

"Have you heard from Eddy?"

"Don't even go there, Julia, you can't fix everything."

I recoiled from her bitterness but took a breath and looked more carefully at her. "You look exhausted. Do you want to go to the bedroom and lie down for a while? I can easily manage these two. Just maybe feed Damien before you go, then I won't have to disturb you."

Donna's expression was hungry. "Well . . . but what I'd really love is to get out on my own for an hour or two. Do you think I could leave him here with you?" Her face crumpled, near tears. "I just feel like I'm going mad."

"Sure. Whatever you need."

123

Donna fed him. It was difficult to watch, seeing Damien look to Donna for her smile and Donna resisting, sometimes drawn in, then pulling away. "Parasite," she said, softly.

He needed changing but I told her to go. Donna took a jar from her bag and put it on the kitchen bench. "If he gets hungry, he's on solids now, you can give him this. He likes it better warm but don't worry if that's extra bother. Or just throw him some bread to gnaw on, that might keep him quiet." She dropped him back in his car seat and headed for the door, turning briefly. "Thanks a million, J."

Bent at the middle so soon after feeding, Damien's face screwed up almost immediately. I picked him up and rubbed his back for a few minutes, staring into space and thinking about Donna. He became smiley and charming, then started reaching for things over my shoulder. "Bored, huh?"

I lay him on his back under Maria's play frame and watched as he contentedly batted and swung the bright objects. After a while he began pulling his head up. I fetched a cushion to put behind him and propped him into a sitting position. Here he gurgled and grinned, toppling over sideways once or twice, but soon finding his balance. I realised I had rarely seen him out of his car seat and he was nearly seven months old.

Simon laughed when he came home and found me carrying two babies and setting cold food out on the table at the same time. "You should have ten children, just to fully exploit your talents as a mother. Where's Donna?"

"I don't honestly know. She went out for a couple of hours, but that was before lunch. She's not answering her texts. I guess she'll be back soon."

Simon kissed Maria and began to take her off my arm. "Actually, would you take this one instead? He keeps wriggling and I'm worried I'll drop him. Sit on the floor and show him some cars. This is nearly done, there's bread in the oven. I'll change Maria and we can eat."

Donna came in soon after, looking guilty but relaxed. "Sorry. Was he okay?" I was relieved to see her go to Damien and pick him up with a smile. "Who'd have thought I'd miss you?"

28

I had planned to go back to the café after a few months, but very soon I knew I would not leave Maria. Carl wasn't surprised. "Keep in touch, Love?"

The furniture was beginning to sell a little better, and some days I was rushed to get it all done. Work on the house was slow and I modified my plans to keep the renovations simpler, deciding to recoat the existing bath and just replace the shower rather than do the whole bathroom, and painting the kitchen cupboards, putting on new handles to sharpen it up. It all got easier as Maria got older. Once she could crawl I let her follow me from room to room, picking her up only when she got tired, or was interested in something above her all-fours vision. It was a challenge to keep all the paints and tools safely out of the way, but progress accelerated and I began to feel I was heading somewhere again.

It was a clear, cool morning. Simon helped me load the furniture onto a trailer before he left for work.

"How will you manage when you get there, and with Maria?"

"Martin will help, it'll be fine."

I pulled into the parking area at the back of the shop and knocked on the back door. It was a while before Martin appeared.

"Sorry, customer. Hey, great! Let's put these three into the van, I'll deliver them straight out. And the others in the shop."

I brought Maria in and spent some time with Martin, adjusting the display to make room for the new furniture, trying things in various arrangements until I was satisfied. "It has to look great from the door, and from the window, so people want to come in. And the best pieces should be in the simplest eye-lines, so they are what people see first – here, come to the door and look."

"Julia, you're a genius! Marry me and run the shop?"

I laughed. "How's it going with Nora?"

Martin sighed. "It's like pulling teeth to get her to go out with me. I think I should give up, she just isn't really interested."

"Keep trying; I know you two are right for each other."

"She says she doesn't know why I bother, that she's too dull to be good company – but I keep telling her, I love spending time with her, so maybe it's just a nice way of saying she finds me boring."

"No, Martin, honestly, that's not it. She's been low with her job, but she's not always like that. Please, don't give up. Please?"

He put his hands up, "Hey, okay, I'm persuaded. Now, new order."

"So soon?"

"Yup."

"Tell me."

Before I left, I went back to the car for Martin's invoice. He took it from me. "It would help if I paid it now, right?"

"Martin, you're a saint! Yes, please. And come over to dinner this weekend, I'll invite Nora, too."

As soon as I had one child, I knew I wanted more. Talking about it brought up all the old issues between Simon and me and we couldn't agree. We were arguing about it one afternoon when Nora phoned.

"Hey it's me. Have you heard from Donna?"

"Not for a few days. Why, what's up?" I felt a cold dread fall into my stomach. Donna had a new boyfriend, worse than the last. "Kevin?"

"Yeah . . . I think it's got pretty bad. And now I can't get hold of her. I told her she should come to me, or that you'd have her . . . sorry Julia . . ."

"No, of course."

"But she looked hunted, I couldn't get her to agree to anything, or even acknowledge there was a problem."

"You phoned?"

"There's no answer."

"Anywhere else she could have gone?"

"I gave her the number for the Women's Refuge. But I told her to phone to let me know what she was doing."

"Well, you know Donna. She makes questionable decisions but generally she's pretty good at looking after herself."

Nora said nothing.

"Are you really worried?"

"Yeah. Something doesn't feel right."

"Okay, I'll go round. If I can't find her, I'll talk to the police."

"Police!"

"Just leave it to me."

The outside of the property was a mess, the garden dead in parts with some voracious weeds overgrowing, rubbish all around. I knocked on the door and got no answer. I looked in the windows, there was mess everywhere. I had just seen that Damien's cot was empty when there was a shout from inside. "Fuck off, witch!" I raced to the car and drove away, shaking, cursing my cowardice.

"Nora, give me that Refuge number. I'll call them."

"I've already tried. They can't tell me where she is, or even if she's there. I get why, but . . ."

I talked to the police and explained my concerns. "She may have gone to the Refuge, or somewhere else, and if she has, it's not surprising she hasn't called us. But we're worried something worse may have happened."

Two hours later I got a call back. "Mrs Davis? Hi. Look, we know where she is, and she's okay."

"Can you tell me where? I'd like to see her."

"I'm sorry, no, not without her permission."

"Okay. Well, thanks, I really appreciate what you've done."

Nora was angry at Donna. "Worrying us like this. Why wouldn't she come to us, or at least call?"

"She knows we're here, and when she feels better she'll remember we love her. Just give her time."

I let out my frustration when Simon came home. "Men! What is it about these guys that they need to control women? Right from the start he didn't like her going out without him, wanted Damien raised with his rules; and he hated me. Why are men like this?"

Simon stood up and walked around the table, taking me by both arms. I wondered what he was doing. His pupils were like pinheads. "'Men' are not like this! You are talking about one man, or a string of them, if you look at the idiots and psychopaths Donna is attracted to. Don't talk as if we were all the same."

I shook my head impatiently. "Of course I don't mean you!"

"Then don't say 'men' like that. There's this odd assumption I make, that if you say something, you mean it. I'm not Kevin, I'm not your father and I'm not Lance. Why can't you just trust me? It's infuriating."

I looked at him for a long moment. I heard him consciously but in my heart his words made no sense. "I'm sorry. I'm listening, but I keep thinking about Donna. I just wish I could help her."

"Maybe you can't. Letting her know what you thought of Kevin didn't work much magic, remember?"

I nodded. She still wasn't speaking to me.

"You can't fix everything, Julia."

"Funny, that's exactly what she said."

29

We took time out for a holiday at the beach. It was the week before Christmas, before most of the holidaymakers arrived. The house we stayed in had a wide view of the sea. Maria had just started walking and planted her face in the sand more than once. Simon and I would comfort her and get the sand out of her mouth and seconds later she would be laughing again and toddling off once more.

Simon leaned back. "I love it here, and being completely away from everything. Maybe we should buy a place like this."

I noted the "we". My feet shuffled and I looked into the distance. "Being away always makes me want to make plans. I've been thinking of maybe stepping up the business, or perhaps starting something new."

"But you're barely keeping up now."

I grimaced. "Things change. Anything's possible. Or maybe I should work out how to finance another house; the potential gain there is much bigger than I can get from doing furniture on my own."

"You want to move?"

"Not necessarily; maybe stay there and do something smaller, faster; it would be easier without living in it. But admit it, the house is much better than you imagined it could be when you first saw it."

Simon shrugged uneasily. Maria fell and began to grizzle again. "Shall we go back up for lunch?"

My planning faded as I came down with 'flu towards the end of the week. I was glad to get home.

"I'm never sick," I whimpered on the fourth day of not being able to lift my head from the pillow. I came out of it in time for New Year, but something of the nausea lingered; it was only when I was progressively more sick a week later that I began to wonder what was going on.

I sat at the table while Maria slept and stared at nothing. Thoughts circled around in my mind.

Simon came in.

"Sit down. I need to tell you something."

He pulled out a chair and waited without speaking.

"I didn't plan this, but I'm pregnant."

Simon nodded but said nothing.

"No reaction – tell me what you're thinking."

"You don't want to hear it."

"Tell me anyway."

"I think it's time we got married."

I sighed. "This doesn't change anything. It was an accident."

"Getting married would hardly change anything, either. It makes sense."

"I don't want to get married for 'sense'."

"Julia, I've told you I love you in every way I know how. And you love me."

"Of course I . . . Look, I don't really understand it myself, but I feel like I'm fighting for my life even thinking about it . . ."

How could I tell him that every time I thought seriously about marrying him I had dreams about Lance? Nightmares full of derisive laughter and scorn. "Can't make it on your own, Baby? Need a man to look after you?"

Later, just before bed, I went to where Simon was reading and knelt down beside him. "I'm just so scared."

"Why? I don't understand."

"Can't you just be happy with the way things are?"

"Is it Lance?"

I knew what it took for him to ask me. "Maybe. But not that I love him more than you. I think I'm scared that if I let myself go, let myself trust this, that something will happen. Something will go wrong."

"I'm not going to die."

"I know. I know it consciously . . ." I closed my eyes, fighting back tears.

"Darling, please . . ." but he could not let go of it. "You need to work this out, maybe a counsellor . . ?"

"No." I laughed without humour. "Forget this, it's probably hormones and I've been sick as a dog." I closed my eyes. "I'm tired now."

Simon pulled back and I grabbed at his arm to keep him close. "Okay," he whispered. "Okay."

Three weeks later I was still sick. Simon was going on a business trip. He stood at the bathroom door. "Julia, my taxi will be here in twenty minutes. We need to resolve this."

"I'm puking up the soles of my feet. We'll do it when you get back."

"But that's a month, and then it will be another month, I know you."

"You're not listening to me!" I called, then retched again.

"And you don't see my side at all, ever."

"I'm trying, Simon, but just for now, fuck off."

When I came out Simon was gone, his bags were gone. I sat down and sobbed.

Five days later I lay in hospital, weak from loss of blood and blank with grief. "Bring me my phone."

"You're not supposed to use it," Nora answered.

"Just bring it."

I didn't know if Simon's phone would work in England, if he even had it with him, but I sent the text anyway.

"Why don't you call him, speak to him?"

"No."

"Or I will."

"No. He won't accept it coming from you."

"What is it? What does it say?"

I flicked the screen back.

> I've miscarried, so it was all for nothing.
>
> Did we bring this on ourselves?
>
> I don't want you back. J.

Nora closed her eyes and put her hand to her mouth. I took the phone from her and turned it off. I didn't want to know if he replied.

The day I went home Simon called. It was a conversation with long silences. "Did you mean it? Nora sent an email telling me the state you were in, with the drugs and the pain."

"I don't know, I thought I did."

"Anyway, whether you did or not, I think maybe it's for the best. I want something more in my life than this uncertainty. And unless something changes . . . Will it?"

"I don't know. Maybe I'm fatally independent."

"Fatally . . . that's an appropriate word. Well, I've waited as long as I can. Bye, Julia."

30

Two weeks later, there was an unexpected knock on the front door. "It's open," I called, and Nora came in. "Hey, Babe. How are you?"

"Hi. Good time?"

"Horrible, so I'm glad to see you."

"What's up?"

"I'm just facing the fact that without Simon helping with the bills – don't look at me like that, Nora – I can't afford to stay here. I'm going to have to sell the house, free up the capital and live more simply."

"You live pretty simply as it is."

"Well, somewhere smaller then, rent somewhere while I regroup."

"But you're happy here."

"We'll be happy somewhere else. And we need to eat."

"But the furniture? It's doing well."

"Sure, I sell all I make. But I can only make so much."

"Well, get someone to help, employ someone."

"It's not that easy. Each piece takes hours." I sighed. "And I couldn't have someone under foot here."

Nora didn't reply, waiting for me to continue.

"I suppose I might find someone like me who wanted some work to do at home, but the space it takes! Although if they had a garage . . . And maybe we can streamline things; I do one piece at a time, but if someone were doing several pieces the same, if they only did one sort . . . There are other things I've been thinking about, but haven't had time to do . . ."

Nora was a great sounding-board, listening mostly, asking the occasional guiding question. She made herself a cup of coffee and sat down, handing me paper so I could write down my ideas. Finally I grabbed her hands and danced around the room with her. "You are a genius!" I shouted, "We can stay here, and I can begin building an empire. I don't know why I had been thinking so small."

Nora laughed. "Me, either. Hey, big news! Martin and I are getting married."

I threw my head back and punched my hands in the air. "Yes! What did I say?"

Nora grinned. "Okay, okay, you were right. I'll leave you in charge of my romantic life from now on. Whenever I need a husband, I'll come to you."

"But you're happy? You have no reason to marry him if he's not perfect."

"Oh, Julia, after all you've been through, setting this up? I'm teasing. Don't worry, this is right."

We danced again. "I was SO ready for some good news. Do I get to be bridesmaid? I'll even wear a ghastly floral dress, if that's what you want."

Nora put a hand on her cheek. "Well, it's funny you should ask, because I was thinking, little Austrian costumes, with bells attached to little goatskin purses." We giggled like school girls.

"Time to celebrate. There's a bottle of champagne in the fridge which Simon and I bought for something, but I couldn't drink it while I was pregnant. It's been there like a hex, reminding me of how quickly things went wrong . . . Oh, pah! Back on track, phone Martin, he should be here, too."

"It's 10:30."

"He'll be up, or wake him."

I paced backwards and forwards as I waited for Simon to arrive to take Maria for the afternoon. Her bag was packed since yesterday, but every few passes through the hall I opened it again and peered in, checking and rechecking various items at random. Maria had got my handbag and was pulling out keys and tissues and lipsticks but I barely knew what she was doing, just grateful she wasn't calling for my attention. I watched through the side window as he drove up and my heart beat hard as he walked up the path. He knocked and I fought for breath before opening the door.

"Hi." I looked for his familiar eyes but found only coldness. I had heard it on the phone, but this was a shock.

Maria hadn't seen him for six weeks and her face split into a huge grin. "Daddy!" She tripped and fell headlong towards him. We both ran to pick her up. She reached out of my arms and grabbed him around the neck. I felt his leg against mine as we knelt on the floor.

"Hey, Honey, do you want to come and see Grandma?"

The image of the three of them together flashed like a sword blade.

I stood up and took the bag from the console table. Simon stayed on the floor, arms tight around Maria. I needed something to do so I didn't have to watch them. "I'll get Ruby." I went to fetch her favourite doll from her bedroom, taking a moment to collect myself before returning. He was already at the door, backlit by the sunlight.

"Don't go yet." I couldn't see his face clearly.

"Got something else to say?"

"Sorry. I'm sorry. It was just that I needed . . ."

"There is nothing you can tell me about what you thought you needed that I don't know."

I searched for words for long seconds. "How can that be when I don't understand it myself?"

He turned to go, his hand on the doorknob, then turned back. "You keep digging inside your own mind for answers but you'll never find them until you see into the hearts and minds of others. You are utterly selfish. That's why you feel alone."

The truth of his words impacted my body but my mind shielded itself against them. He watched me shake and turn, and I saw a flicker of concern as he made a stunted movement towards me.

"I'll see you at four," I heard myself say as I groped into the living room, feeling for a sofa to fall onto. The seconds before the door closed were very, very long.

I heard the car drive away and I felt like I was dying. I had left Maria with him many times before, but that was when I knew him, and when I knew myself.

31

I interviewed people to work from home on furniture, mostly mothers wanting a few hours' work to fit in with children. They were well qualified, women with experience in many areas, but the flexibility was everything and they were excited.

It made sense to divide the work, one doing preparation, another priming, another painting. I did the finishing myself, and taking the pieces from one worker to another allowed me to check the quality of the work. At first I hired trailers but soon it became obvious I should buy one. I looked at several from the newspaper, in the end paying a lot for a clean and tidy covered furniture trailer, so I didn't need to wait for good weather. I was absurdly proud of it, taking my friends outside to show it to them. I was thinking of having a logo put on it, on the sides and back.

"Fantastic idea!" said Nora. "Time to take things to the next level, get professional."

I had been running as a sole trader and done my own tax, but it was time to get an accountant, and register a company. I longed to talk to Simon but Nora and Martin were the next best thing. They came over for coffee in the dead hours of Saturday afternoon, when I missed Maria most.

This time she was staying overnight with Simon. I had packed and repacked her bags, sick at the thought of spending the night without her. I kept my smile glued on as I handed her through the door, waved her down the path. I was too ashamed to say more than a few words to Simon.

I baked biscuits to fill the time before Martin and Nora arrived, then collected paper and pens for our brainstorm.

Pretty soon things were running smoothly. I discovered who worked quickly and who was best on non-urgent jobs. Sally was excellent at priming and painting but left rough patches when she worked on preparation and sanding. Lisa tended to leave brush marks that were hard to cover. I worked with them to improve the quality, but where possible coordinated their strengths and preferences. I learned to give an approximate timescale, and asked them to call me if they couldn't meet it. Production was even quicker and more efficient than I had expected, especially once I taught Sally to do some of the finishing work and found someone else to work on the earlier tasks. A lot of my own time now was spent on administration.

Nora came over to talk about the wedding, and after that we discussed business. "It's thriving. For the first time in ages we could make more than I am currently selling. It's such a relief."

"So will you try to sell more?" Nora put away the samples of bridesmaids' fabrics and settled back on the sofa with her tea.

"Well, yes, but I'm thinking what to do. I think the local market has enough of what we are doing at the moment, but there might be some other things we could try. I've been looking through magazines, to see what is current that we could have a go at."

"And?"

"And I'm still thinking. But I feel excited, ready to go, make a big leap, not sure to what. There's a business course on expansion which I thought I'd go to. Just have to get someone to take Maria."

"Aunt Nora?"

"Are you sure?"

"When is it?"

I had distantly noticed the phenomenon before, that when I put energy into the business I got results that were apparently unrelated. I came back from the course full of ideas, and had started putting together marketing material and made a few phone calls, when completely outside my current effort I received a message from a buyer in Auckland. I sent up pictures and pricelists, called some freight companies to work out delivery costs, and the result was an order bigger than any I had had before. Near the end of the panic to get that done, a new exclusive bed and breakfast in the Southern Lakes called.

"We're working to a tight schedule, want to launch before the summer tourist season, and House and Garden are going to do a feature in the October issue."

"What do you need, exactly?"

"Furniture for twelve rooms: bed, bedside tables, drawers and wardrobe. And some dressers and sideboards for the public areas. In three weeks? We'll get you a mention in the article if that helps. No-one else is doing what you are."

I took Maria down to with me to look at the building. It was set in the mountains, rock facing on the outside walls and a slate roof. Some of the rooms were still unlined, but the owners were sure it would be ready on time. "Just wiring to finish, and painting, which has started. It's not as bad as it looks."

"I can see it, it's gorgeous, and I'm so happy to be involved."

32

I was overflowing with it when Simon arrived on the Saturday, and the focus on something positive gave me courage to ask him in.

"Time for a coffee?"

He raised an eyebrow but nodded and followed me through the hall, standing awkwardly until I invited him to sit. I told him about the new opportunities.

"I'm pleased for you, Julia, you deserve it, you've worked so hard." So distant. I wanted to cry.

"Listen . . ."

He was still, almost inanimate, then raised his hands impatiently. "What?"

"I've thought about what you said. You were right. I've been trying to understand how you felt, and I'm sorry I hurt you. Can you forgive me?"

"The hurt's forgotten, or it will be."

"But you're angry."

"I'm angry about the broken promise."

I honestly didn't know what he was talking about.

"You promised Maria would be mine, too. Then you took her away."

"We split up. It was nothing to do with Maria."

"You took away my life with my child."

I stared at him in horror as his words sank in. His gaze was steady, and so, so angry. I opened my mouth to speak.

"Don't say anything, Julia. There's nothing you can say that will make a difference."

I buried my guilt in my work. Getting the bed and breakfast order together was exhausting. The dressers were new items for us and the shells weren't delivered until ten days to go. That was just long enough but in the worry about that there was a mix-up with the ordering and I found we were out of stock of bedside tables. Once they arrived I was up all night more than once but as the deadline approached I didn't see how we would be ready. I dreaded making the phone call to say I was letting them down.

Even when I wasn't working I didn't sleep well. I was short-tempered with everyone and feeling so bad about myself it felt like everything was spiralling down. My hot angry tears got in the way of the finishing work and I threw my brush against the wall after I ruined a final coat on the drawer of a bedside table.

Nora looked up. "Why don't you take a break. You haven't stopped for days." I knew I was being a brat and her saintly patience just made me more resentful.

"I can't, you know that."

"Just go for a walk, ten minutes. You're getting unbearable."

"I said I can't stop! You leave if you don't like it."

She pulled me by the arm towards the door. My frustration found a focus and I shrugged violently out of her grip. "Let me go!"

I don't know what I would have done if Maria hadn't appeared at the door. "Mummy. Not shout!"

"Ten minutes," ordered Nora.

"All right! Fine."

It was a short block and I walked around it twice, my breathing becoming steadier, thoughts becoming clear. I walked back into the house. Nora was attempting to read a book to Maria who was sitting on her knee turning the pages too quickly.

"I'm going to have to call them. We're not ready."

"What if we got more help?"

"Paint still takes a certain amount of time to dry. And I'm the bottleneck, I can't train someone to do what I do in two days. We're not ready."

I hated the sense of failure as I picked up the phone, but the sooner I told them the better.

I interpreted the silence at the end of the line as disappointment and broken trust and my cheeks dragged downwards. "Are you there?"

"Yeah, I'm just thinking. Two days more, you said? Is anything ready?"

"Yes, it's just the smaller bedroom stuff. The sideboards and cupboards are done."

"Okay, cool. Why don't you send those, we can set them up, and maybe we can get a van to bring the small things later."

I realised how I had lost perspective. It was obvious. "I can bring them myself, on the trailer."

"Great! Then you can help us arrange everything. That's perfect."

I was so relieved and so proud. The guest rooms looked bare when I arrived at the hotel, but once we put the final pieces in and placed lamps and vases, they were immediately finished.

I watched Sophia, the House and Garden journalist, take photographs, styling as she went, moving bowls of flowers, opening or closing curtains and blinds to get the light right, taking shots from unexpected angles. "Usually I know which will work and which won't, but I always take a few wildcards, and sometimes I'm surprised." She complimented me on the furniture. "I'd love some myself, but I travel so much I've never found time for a place of my own."

The idea intrigued me, it sounded so free. "You don't feel the need for security?"

"It's not that, I just don't think a house gives you security."

"A novel idea! I've always thought the bigger the better."

"Security doesn't come from people or things, it comes from trusting yourself."

We were sitting on the veranda with a bottle of wine. I raised my glass. "Well then, here's to trusting ourselves." And then to the owners. "Good luck! I'm envious. It's something I'd never have been brave enough to do."

"Well, for our sakes, stick to what you are doing, at least for a while. The furniture is great."

"Hear, hear."

I looked out at the view again, into the far distance of the mountains, blue in the twilight. I felt my chest expand. "You know, I want to savour this moment, but there's part of me that knows it will pass, and is desperate to hold onto it."

Sophia had been holding her glass up to the horizon, playing with the distorted image. She closed one eye and tilted her head to the side. "Moments like this happen every hour of every day. You just have to notice."

Her words rang out into the silence.

33

"Hi, Julia? It's me. Listen, there's something I want to ask."

It had happened, Simon had met someone. He hadn't introduced her to Maria and he wanted to do it at home, where she would feel at ease. Shit, I thought, am I up to this?

Thank goodness the House and Garden article was out that week, too, to give me another focus. I put the magazine on the coffee table in case I was lost for something to say, then went to the kitchen to keep myself busy.

At three, I placed a plate of cheese straws on the end of the counter and paced back and forth twice. I looked down at my hands, which were wringing each other, and shook them to my sides. "Get a grip," I said out loud. "You knew this would happen." I struggled to control a surge of jealousy, but had not quite achieved it when there was a knock at the door. Both fists clenched briefly as I walked over. I opened it, and there Ellen stood. I didn't register Simon, looked past him with a sinking heart. She's beautiful . . .

Ellen was nervous, closed off with her hands together in front of her, holding her bag. She was formal in powder-blue skirt and jacket. High heeled shoes. Perfect makeup, perfect hair in a blonde chignon, perfect nails. "She works for an airline," Simon had told me. "Cabin crew." She was tall and held herself straight, controlled like a dancer.

I put out my hand. "Ellen, I've been so looking forward to meeting you, come in." Simon stepped back and Ellen looked to him for support before coming forward. He put his arm around her shoulder as she passed and followed close behind. I felt sick, bile rising to my mouth. My eyes went dark for a moment and I closed them. Get a grip. Deal with these emotions later. Simon was looking at me, an odd expression on his face, as if nervous about what I would do next. Somewhere I found a smile.

"Please, sit down. Let me get you something to drink." I brought the plate of biscuits to the coffee table and placed them near Ellen, who was perched on the front of the sofa, her bag on her knee. "Tea, coffee?"

"Yes, please."

I raised an eyebrow at Simon.

"We'll both have tea, black for me, and milk, no sugar." I felt Ellen's gaze on me as I walked back to the kitchen.

"Where is Maria?" Simon asked.

I looked up and called through the hall door. "Maria, Daddy's here."

There was a thunder of footsteps, cries of "Daddy, Daddy" and the brittle tension scattered as Maria hurtled into the room, curls flying, and wrapped herself around Simon's legs. Simon crouched down next to her. "Darling, this is Ellen, a friend of mine." Ellen smiled; I was surprised at the warmth in her face after the nervous coldness of her entrance.

"Maria, how lovely to meet you." Maria looked at me, at Simon, then, as Ellen crouched down too and held out her hand, she stepped towards her. "Who have you got there?"

Maria held out the toy she was holding. "This is Po. I love her."

Ellen laughed, and took the small doll. "She looks beautiful," she said, running her hand over her before handing her back.

"Mummy, Mummy, DVD!" Maria cried.

"Maybe later."

"Do you have any other toys?"

"Yes! Yes!" Maria took Ellen by the hand and tugged her towards the bedroom.

"Do you mind?" she asked me. Her smile was still shy, but warmer.

"Of course . . ." I waved towards the door. Ellen allowed Maria to lead her out.

I sagged back against the bar. "Oh, Simon."

"Are you all right?"

I forced a nod. "Of course, of course. You know I . . . she's lovely, quite beautiful."

He tilted his head to the side and back in reluctant acknowledgement. Our eyes met briefly and something in me relaxed. He doesn't love her, I realised. Thank God! I picked up the teapot and put it down again.

Simon came over. "Here, let me make that. Are you having one?"

The House and Garden article had its effect and within days we were busy again with new orders. I had tried to anticipate what we might need and we had a few complete bedroom sets made up. Storage had been becoming an issue, but now everything flew out as we tried to keep up with demand. At the same time, I was developing new ideas so that when the current style inevitably went out of vogue we would have other things coming through.

Maria's speech was becoming more fluent and I heard Ellen's name frequently. More and more, the happy family image came into my mind: Simon, beautiful Ellen, Maria. Each time I went cold. I needed to take control, make some gesture of acknowledgement of Ellen's place in Maria's life. I took a deep breath and invited them to dinner.

"Are you sure?" Simon's expression was perplexed. "Of course, I'd like Maria to see us all friends."

"Of course."

Nora and Martin came, too, for moral support. Everything was fine until I was setting out plates in the kitchen, and suddenly glanced up and froze, knowing something had changed. Ellen was talking to Martin, and Maria was running from Nora to Simon and back again. The image etched itself in my mind, Simon absently patting Maria on the head, apparently listening to Nora, ear inclined towards her but his eyes and attention fixed on Ellen. Love. He was in love with her, euphoric infatuation breaking out of his habitual calm.

He had not been like this last time I saw them together, but that was two months ago. Things had changed. In my mind the moment lengthened. Maria ran into my leg, and when I looked back, Ellen was raising her gaze to Simon's. She met it - I realised with surprise - reserved, quiet Ellen met it playfully, with the same sparking intensity. She poked out her tongue at him and, irresistibly, laughed.

I went back to serving and swallowed. Well, what did I expect?

I passed a tormented night, filled with images of them together. I hadn't been jealous of Ellen's beauty or, before now, of their time together. But now he loved her. I'd been a fool.

34

Simon came to pick up Maria next morning. Ellen wasn't with him but I had the feeling he'd just got out of bed. He stood inside the door, waiting for Maria to choose some toys, not fully there. I stood to one side of him, where I could watch him unobserved, but he wouldn't have noticed anyway. I felt a strong tug, from deep inside my chest, to touch him, call him back to me. I reached out and put a hand on his shoulder, but just as I made contact he crouched to help Maria with the straps on her backpack. He turned upwards as he registered the touch, looked questioningly, then picked up Maria, clinging to his neck. "See you this afternoon?"

He was leaving. I put a hand on his free shoulder and looked into his eyes. "Simon?"

He was puzzled. "Yes?" Maria was wriggling.

I shook my head, flexed my lips. "Have a good day."

Simon sat opposite me at the kitchen table and talked about Ellen. My mouth set into a perfectly straight line and I willed my eyes to stay neutral. Fortunately he was not really looking at me, the occasional glances he made at my face were unseeing. He just wanted to talk and the old habit of confiding in me made it easy; but he had never talked so freely, so enthusiastically, when we were together. Fate's revenge.

"You wouldn't believe it, I don't think she's ever been with a man who treated her with respect, or who valued her beyond her looks. She couldn't believe I didn't expect her to sleep with me straight away, or that I'd be willing to spend time with her if she didn't. Men compete for her - well, you've seen her - but just as a trophy, not for herself. I just want to convince her, show her there are decent men, we're not all like the ones she's met."

"Just as well you kept that armour well shined."

He focused on me, finally, as my words caught him. "What?"

"Sorry, don't mind me." I put a hand on his cheek, my fingers burning. "You're sweet. I'm glad to see you in love."

He grinned at this, shook his head. "I'm just so relaxed with her, so . . . free of fear. I know it's an odd declaration, but it's what I feel. It's early yet, but we've talked about getting married."

I breathed in through my nose and after a beat gave a single nod. "Right." I nodded again. Time to let go, I thought. This could be tricky.

Activity, that's what I needed, a big new project.

I looked around. This was a big step, but it felt right. The factory building was dull, but the spaces were good for what I needed, a large workshop area and offices at one end. I would use the boardroom for childcare, with a trained pre-school teacher and the other workers taking turns to help. In the school holidays there were a couple of other rooms which the older children could use, and there was space outside for play equipment.

I turned to the agent. "You're a genius, this is perfect. But offer $100,000 less than they're asking, I think they haven't realised the market has gone quiet the last six months, and it's going to cost a lot to do the alterations."

Now that I needed someone full-time in the office Nora reminded me of my promise. "You said once you were successful you'd give me a job."

"But this is administration work, secretarial, it's not enough for you."

"Look, we're four years on and I'm wasting away in that mindless bureaucracy. I want the job, I really do. Can I have it?"

"Of course, but only until you find something better."

"I'm not looking for something better. I'm going to make this work."

It took some negotiating, and waiting while the owner of the factory realised no better offers were coming, but finally we were in. The loan was terrifying. If there was any delay in getting up and going I would have to sell the house, car, everything I owned.

I organised temporary childcare at my home so all the workers could help with the renovation. We brightened up the lighting, installed skylights, and painted so that it was a fun place to be. Later it would be noisy and smelly, but we did what we could, improving ventilation and putting baffles on the ceiling. Working together we all felt involved. Lisa asked to do a mural on the long wall and Sally suggested a sound system to keep us motivated. Then we started production. I was so proud as I stood watching everyone work, realising how lonely it had been until then, with each of us isolated at home.

The women loved the childcare, knowing the children were nearby so they could be called if necessary. They could visit on breaks, but weren't having to constantly juggle, so they could concentrate on what they were doing, get a task completed without interruption.

Word got out about the arrangements, and we had applications from fathers, too, single parents, week-about, and those whose partners had less accommodating employers. I wondered at first if adding men into the mix would change the dynamics, but why deny them this opportunity? We would deal with whatever issues arose.

Many of the workers finished at three; some started early to make up more hours. Production would wind down a little for the school holidays – the entertainment for the older children would be useful, but they would still need a break, so those parents would take time off, or take work home.

Freed from the logistics of managing all the workers separately, I found time to think about expansion. I was already sending stock to other cities, but hesitated to export, particularly with the exchange rate strong. So what else? I decided to continue doing residential property on a small scale, project managing rather than doing the work myself, and with investors, since I didn't want to take on more loans until the factory was reliably funding itself.

At the same time as I was looking for another house to buy, I got a call from *The Press* newspaper wanting to do an article on the new work environment. I asked the staff, who all enthusiastically agreed to show the journalist around and talk to him. In the midst of it all, Nora suggested applying for a business award. She and I did the application together and we won. It was all very encouraging, and it helped balance what I was still feeling about Simon.

35

Simon. The wedding was this week, and somehow I had managed to keep it out of my thoughts. Ellen had taken Maria for her dress – good luck to her, getting Maria to walk up the aisle scattering flowers as planned, but that was her decision, her problem. I was taking Maria tonight to the rehearsal, and had offered to stay and help explain to her what she was expected to do.

Tension was high when we walked into the church. Ellen was whispering furiously to a couple of older women. Simon came over and spoke in a low voice to me.

"Thanks for coming."

"What's going on?"

"I'm not sure, something about the flowers, best I stay out."

"Weddings, eh? Bring out the best in everyone."

Simon laughed. "It's great to see you, I feel like we haven't talked in ages."

Something made me look up, straight into Ellen's furious expression, her eyes fixed sharply on us. "I think you're needed."

I stayed, but felt uneasy. Ellen's gaze was often on me during the rest of the rehearsal. I pointed the way and led Maria, finally suggesting Simon bribe her with a sweet in his pocket. "Just for goodness sake, don't forget it!"

Maria couldn't understand the rehearsal concept, and didn't see why there were no petals in her basket. I kept repeating "Tomorrow" but she became upset. It was past her bedtime. Simon came over to help and took her on a tour of the church. I sat down at the end of a pew.

"Can I have a word?" Ellen hissed.

I looked up, surprised. I stood and followed her to a quiet corner.

"Just what is it with you and Simon? He says you are just friends now, sharing responsibility for Maria, but I saw you before. And he's always talking about you."

I paused, searching for a reply. "He's marrying you."

Ellen tapped her foot irritably. "Not a good answer."

"I can see how you feel. It looks complicated, but it really isn't. I'd probably feel the same if I were you, but I was not the one for Simon, we both know it."

"Who both?"

"Simon and me. And you should trust it, too." I put my hand on Ellen's arm, to reassure her. "Really. Be happy. It's going to be a wonderful day."

Ellen looked like she was about to crumple. "I'm just not sure I'll be able to cope."

Maria was wild to see Simon after the two-week honeymoon and was jumping up and down at the door. Uncharacteristically, he was late collecting her, and subdued when he got there.

"Hi. Hey, what do you think about going to the playground this morning?"

I was surprised, usually he liked to take her straight home, and go out later. "Ellen's working today?" He had mentioned she was.

His expression was wary. "No, she called in sick. She says she needs some time to get over the stress of the wedding."

Two weeks on an idyllic island wasn't enough? I bit my tongue.

"Anyway, she needs a little quiet, so I said I'd let her rest."

I had a moment of foreboding. "Listen, if you need to bring Maria back early, I'll be here."

"Thanks. But we'll be fine." Our eyes met in a moment of nearly honest regret. "I adore Ellen. She just needs someone to look after her."

"Well, I'm here," I repeated, and went to fetch Maria's sunhat.

Simon phoned one Sunday in March. "Hi, Julia, listen, would you come and pick Maria up this afternoon? I've got a business trip, one of our guys got sick halfway through a tradeshow, and I need to get there straight away – I'm leaving this afternoon."

"Sure. Do you want me to come now?"

"No, I'm packing, the taxi's coming at two. But Ellen will be fine for a while, so come any time."

I avoided seeing Simon and Ellen together when I could help it. "Okay, I won't get in your way while you're getting ready. I'll come around two thirty."

Ellen and Maria were watching a DVD when I arrived. It was almost over, so I stood back to wait. There was a nearly finished painting on an easel in the corner. "Hey, is this yours?" Ellen nodded. "I didn't know you painted."

"It's nothing, really, just a hobby. Since I stopped work this gives me something to do."

So Ellen wasn't working any more. I looked back at the picture; the scene was outside a café, sunshine and umbrellas.

"It's gorgeous. Just makes me want to sit down and order a coffee."

Ellen smiled. "Grab a drink, this is nearly over."

I looked around the apartment. It was weird being here again. I swallowed, felt the urge to leave. "Do you mind if I sit on the balcony?"

"Go ahead."

This was better, fresh air and a view to distract me. Soon Maria came running out and it was time to go.

I asked Simon about Ellen's painting. "Would she sell me a couple? I have a house coming ready I want to put on the market, and her style is just right."

Simon was pleased. "Ask her."

But Ellen was reluctant. "No, they're not good enough. I wish they were, that I had real talent. But I just paint for us, for friends."

"Not for me?"

"Not to sell. But I'm working on one for Simon's birthday, so I couldn't at the moment anyway."

Something didn't feel quite right, but I didn't push it further.

These weird drop-offs and pick-ups - I both looked forward to them and hated them. Usually I tried to prepare something in advance to say. Today it was easy, it was Simon's birthday. I greeted him at the door with a small parcel in my hand. "Here's a little something from me."

"You didn't have to. I'm embarrassed."

"Don't be, it's nothing."

He opened it: a photo frame with a picture of Maria. "Thanks."

"Did you like Ellen's present?"

"Yeah, see, I'm wearing it." He held out his arms, looking down at a new shirt.

"No, I meant the painting."

A guarded expression crossed Simon's face. "No, that didn't work out. She was upset, she said she couldn't get it right."

"I'm so sorry. But she must know that nothing is ever perfect, that if you look at anything too long, you see faults. Couldn't she . . ?" I stopped as Simon held up his hand. An expression like a shrug passed over his face. He blinked twice.

"Anyway, she says she doesn't want to paint any more, it's too stressful. She might take up photography."

It was none of my business, but it made me impatient to see anyone wasting talent. I bit my thumbnail, tapped my foot and looked for something neutral to say. "Well, she has an eye for anything visual, she'll be brilliant."

Simon nodded gratefully. "She'll start with my camera, then we'll get something better once she gets going."

"She said she's given up work."

Our eyes met, Simon daring me to say more. "That's right. I'm glad. I don't need her to work, and we don't need the money. And now with the baby, it's great she'll be home."

"Baby?"

"Yeah."

I fought back my reaction. "Simon, that's excellent news. Please tell Ellen I'm delighted."

Simon nodded. His voice was wistful. "I just want her to be happy."

36

I sat in front of the computer on a Saturday afternoon feeling for the glands in my neck, which were swollen with the start of a cold. A tense dread had been creeping up as we got closer to this month's loan payment and the income I had prayed for hadn't arrived. I turned it every way but the problem looked impossible. I just wanted to crawl under the duvet and hide.

I looked out at the low, grey sky; it seemed appropriate. It was cold but I had to move.

"Maria!"

She toddled through from her bedroom holding a neon pink bear with a ring of lipstick around its mouth. What had she been up to?

"Come on, we're going out. Let's find your gloves."

Wrapped in layers of wool and fleece and bribed with a box of crackers to hold, Maria submitted to being strapped into her push chair. I walked fast, running from my worries. My cell phone rang in my pocket more than once but I ignored it. I wanted to scream, felt completely trapped. Perhaps I could borrow more, but with that thought the cage only seemed smaller.

On my second circuit around the park I finally had a clear thought. Get help. Ask Martin. I slowed to a stop. Maria turned to look at me and her box of crackers fell to the ground, spilling. She began to cry. "Okay, Honey. Let's go and see Aunty Nora."

I found Martin at the shop, just closing up. He nodded as I unloaded my problem. "Let's talk. There's always a solution."

"Really?" I felt tears forming and a dead weight on my chest.

"Come on. No need for that. You'll be fine. Actually Nora had mentioned this to me already. I've been giving it some thought. I think she's home. I'll let her know we're coming."

Nora put out bruschetta and I realised I hadn't eaten since breakfast. Not the best way to keep my spirits up. "Thanks, Darling." I reached out and squeezed her hand.

I don't know what had I expected – disgust? censure? – but their faces remained calm.

"It seems pretty simple," Martin said. "Either you find a way to quickly increase your turnover or you get more investment. Which do you want to do?"

My answer was sarcastic. "So it's that easy!"

"Why not? Which do you want?"

I made myself listen, playing his words back, feeling my response to each in my body. "I don't see a way to get more in quickly. I'm tired from trying. And more investment seems like digging a bigger hole. I feel so alone."

"Well, what if you weren't? Have you thought about taking on a partner?"

"No." This was my baby, my business. I didn't want to share it.

"Someone to share the responsibility, maybe do the bits you don't want to do."

Nora chimed in. "Like making sure the money actually works. You know you're best at the creative side."

"It sounds like a fantasy. But I keep hearing that partnerships go bad."

"It's all a matter of expectations." Martin spoke so matter-of-factly.

I got up from the table and paced across the room. "Is it really possible? Where would I find someone?"

"What about right here?"

"You?"

"Yeah, me. I'm a bit of a schmuck but I keep money rolling in pretty well. And Nora's talented, she could be doing way more than she is."

"I keep telling her she should find a better job, somewhere else, something creative."

"No, I mean she has a great head for business. She could be pretty much running the place day-to-day. There is a lot you could do better."

I looked from one to the other, feeling huge relief and a huge sense of failure together. "I feel like such a fool."

Nora came over and took my hand. "Why do you think you have to do everything on your own?"

A low fog settled over me. I imagined myself in a glass bubble, looking out but wrapped in silence. "Let me think about it. You're both so generous," and I made my escape.

It was such an obvious answer but the more I saw the necessity and sense of it, the worse I felt. I went to see Martin at the shop again on Monday. I felt like a truculent toddler, sitting on a low chair with my bottom lip sticking out. Martin laughed.

"But I feel such a failure!" I was almost wailing.

A small snort of breath sounded from his nose. "You're not a failure. It's really simple. You're great at ideas, right?"

"Yeah, I suppose so."

"And you love getting things up and going."

"Yeah."

"Listen, you're a creator. It's a gift. But the last thing a creator should do is try to keep something running by themselves. Let me describe it: you love a new project, new systems, inspiring people with new things; but then you get bored. You stop doing what you know works because it's just too tedious to do it again. You come up with big new ideas to do something that's actually very simple. And then things start falling apart."

I was offended but I couldn't hold in a laugh of recognition. "How do you know all this?"

"I see it, and I read it in a book. Listen, there's no failure, you've started something fantastic. Now, I'm not great at ideas – I can recognise them when I see them, and I know what will work, but thinking of them in the first place, no. So this is an opportunity for me as well. You started the business, now let me make it solid for you, give us all a great income. Otherwise you'll be struggling forever, and beating yourself up for not having it handled. I'm good at this, trust me. You won't have to worry about money any more, and you can turn your creative talent to bigger and better projects. What do you think?"

I turned his words into a vision in my mind's eye. It was so tempting, so liberating. I returned my eyes to his expectant face and felt a smile break out on mine. "Really?"

"Really."

I stood up and threw my arms around him. "I haven't done you credit up till now! You are amazing." I gazed into his eyes for a brief moment before he looked up towards the ceiling, embarrassed.

The shop bell rang and we turned to see Nora in the doorway carrying lunch in brown paper bags. "Anything I should know about?" She looked very grumpy. I ran to her and hugged her, too.

"If he can do what he says he can, he's a genius."

Martin blushed and Nora tilted her head.

Martin coughed. "I was just about to suggest Julia go on a sales trip. You said the new line is not selling as well as it could be – it's time you did something about it. Go to Auckland, establish a bigger market there."

"But there's so much to do here."

"Nora can do it, it's time to pass over everything you can to her."

"What about Maria?" I turned to Nora.

"Ask Simon to have her. We're just talking about a couple of days. Go to Auckland, talk to the shops you already deal with and I'll make up a list of others. Martin's sister lives there, and she's a BIG shopper, she'll know where to try." Still I hesitated. "Just one night, up one day, back the next. Maria will hardly know you've gone."

37

I teased Nora about the aftermath of the trip, six months' worth of orders, and all to be completed as soon as possible. Nora was unmoved. "So we'll have to improve production. There are a few inefficiencies still, and we have room in the workshop for three or four new workers."

"But I don't have time to train them!"

"You don't have to! It's better if the others do it anyway – it helps team building. And they're better in touch with how it works at a detail level now, too."

I was about to argue, then nodded. "You are always right. Talk to me about how we can speed things up."

Another result was less expected. One of the Auckland shop owners called to say he was coming down for a meeting and would like to have dinner.

"Can we make it lunch? I feel like I've hardly seen my daughter lately."

"Sure, I have a gap on Tuesday," Quentin replied.

"Tuesday then. Come and see the factory, and we'll go from there."

Lunch was long and delightful. Quentin had a sharp, dry sense of humour and we had lots in common: he had taken a similar plunge, from furniture maker at twenty-two to store owner at twenty-five. "We have a real presence now. I wanted the feel of a long-term family business, and I love it when people forget we haven't been there for decades." He took a sip of wine. "And you, what you have achieved is impressive, too."

"It's fun, it has always been fun, and I still get a buzz out of walking in and seeing so much happening, with such a good atmosphere. Looking after people's families brings fantastic loyalty, and everyone works incredibly hard."

"You have children of your own?"

"Just one – she's great. She's nearly four. Her father's remarried, with a baby due any day, so she'll have a brother or sister."

"You don't mind?"

"Would I say if I did? Not really, but it's a constant dance of politeness and distance. I still care about Simon, but it was my decision to call it off. I feel it's my responsibility to make sure his wife doesn't feel insecure, and make sure everything works for Maria. Sorry, it's dull."

"It's a common story, but that doesn't make it less complicated."

So he understood it. I was grateful, but that was enough said. I turned the conversation back to him, and the trip he was on.

"Julia, I've been meaning to ask. I know things are changing with the business, so it might not be clear, but are you thinking about moving any time soon?"

The question surprised me – Simon usually kept well out of my decisions. "No, we're settled here and I love that feeling. If things go as well as Martin promised, I have plans to enlarge the house, and I'm thinking about a pool, but we can do that here. Why do you ask?"

"It's just that there's a house down the road Ellen and I are interested in, and I thought it would be good for Maria if we were closer. So I wanted to know whether you were planning to stay. What do you think?"

"I really don't mind, Simon, it's up to you."

I found myself thinking about Quentin from time to time during the next week, and was very pleased to hear from him again a fortnight later. "I'm coming down. Do you have any free time?"

Nora had things working like clockwork in the office and she was writing up manuals for systems, keeping track of orders and production, letting me know where things could potentially fall behind.

"Yeah, I'm pretty much redundant here." Nora poked out her tongue. "Where shall we meet? Shall I pick you up from the airport?"

Quentin kissed me as we met; I noticed his aftershave, and the smell of shampoo.

"Tell me how much time you have. Where do you need to be?"

"Nowhere. I don't have any meetings, I just wanted to see you again."

"Wow, throw me a curve ball! What should I make of that?"

"Nothing. You don't have to read much at all into it if you don't want to. I enjoy your company, and it's a short flight. But can we have dinner as well as lunch?"

"I told Maria I'd be back by three, but I'll take the day off, we can be tourists."

Simon and Ellen went ahead and bought the house down the road, just ten doors away. When I saw Simon walking in the gate with Maria I was pleased; it looked so right. In a year or two she would be able to walk the distance on her own.

"Hi!" I held the door wide. Simon kissed me on the cheek as he shepherded Maria inside. "How's the new house?"

"Oh, you know, boxes everywhere. Ellen's tired, so I thought I'd bring Maria out, let her rest."

"Hey, Daddy, see my dolls' house!" Maria called from the bedroom. He put his head on one side, questioning.

"Sure, go ahead."

That weekend Simon was helping clear up after Maria's birthday party. The silence was bliss after two hours of screaming excitement.

"Can you stay a few minutes? I wanted to run something past you."

"Sure." He sat on the sofa, relaxed and at home. "What is it?"

"I've had a new idea, I wanted to talk to you about it. Can I get you a glass of something?"

"Thanks."

I poured sauvignon blanc and sat down on the coffee table opposite him.

"What's up?"

"There's a house for sale at the end of the street - you know it, the bay villa, back from the road, lots of trees. It's been rented, a bit tired. I thought of doing it up for corporate entertaining, hire it out for meetings. I'm really excited."

"Sounds good. How would it work? Would you do catering? Rooms to sleep?"

"No rooms, but yes, food, we'll do up the kitchen, have a chef on call. But I'm not sure about the location. Do you think people will be willing to come out of town?"

"Sure. We often do off-site meetings, even further out. Parking's the only thing. Is there room?"

"Yeah, there's space out the back, so I can keep the garden at the front."

"I'm almost jealous, a new project. The factory's running smoothly?"

"Yeah, Nora doesn't leave me much to do. So I needed something new."

After Simon left, I sat Maria at the table for a snack – she had been too excited to eat while her friends were there. I put out plates and cups, biscuits and juice.

"Did you have fun at Daddy's last night?"

"Yes."

"What did you do?" I had got into the habit of wanting to see inside that world, but when Maria looked at me quizzically, knowing I wanted something but not knowing how to provide it, I realised it was time to stop. We talked about the shape of her biscuit, why the juice spilled when she poured it, what happened to the biscuit when she dipped it in the juice. This was the conversation she needed.

When she was in bed I straightened a few things, then lay on the sofa with a magazine. Instead of reading I drifted into dreaming: about life, the things I loved doing and plans for the future. Quentin floated in and out of my thoughts and I realised I was smiling.

He asked if I would come up to visit him.

"I don't know."

"Just a weekend. When is Maria with Simon? Or you could bring her."

"Not yet. And Simon has the new baby. Let me get back to you?"

I talked it over with Nora.

"I think it's great. It's time you had a new relationship."

"Don't call it that. We're just friends."

Nora smirked. "Fine. But leave Maria with me, she can stay with us for the night."

"Thanks, but Simon said it's fine to have her as usual. Anyway I think I'll take the last flight back. Staying over would raise questions I'd rather put off for a while."

"Suit yourself."

"Nora! Get that smirk off your face."

Nora laughed. "So many of your talents are wasted being single."

"Nora!" It was almost a shriek. "What can you possibly mean?"

"Look at you! It doesn't take much imagination. I've never known how you manage to keep men at arm's length when you have the effect you do, and now you have let someone that bit nearer, I'm fascinated to see what will happen."

"I have no idea where this is going, if anywhere." I closed my eyes and pulled my head back. "Give me time to get my bearings."

"Julia, just go with it, what is stopping you?"

Tears rose, startling both of us. "Do you think I went through what I went through with Simon just to get caught up again?"

"Hey, Honey, take it easy. I'm sorry, that was thoughtless of me." She stepped nearer and put a hand on my arm.

I took a breath and shook my hair back. "No, you're right, it's normal, it's fun. I should just run with it for a while."

After that, Nora didn't tease me about Quentin, treating me carefully in general until I teased her in return. "Stop fussing and get on with running the business! For heaven's sake, I'm not made of glass."

38

"Maria, get your doll. Daddy will be here in a minute."

Simon's knock on the door came soon after. "Maria's nearly ready, come in."

He sat down, edgy.

"Tough Friday? You look tired. Is work okay?"

"Sure, fine."

"Really? Come on, Simon, you're worried. What is it? Is everything okay at home?"

He rubbed his hands over his eyes and pulled his mouth sideways. "It'll work out. It's just tough just now; the baby doesn't sleep, and you know what it's like with a newborn." There was an awkward moment, denied shared memories. "I'm sure that's all it is, she's just tired, she'll be fine. Did you say Maria was ready? We'd better be getting on."

I went to pack my bag, losing sight of Simon in my nervousness about this weekend. I had decided to stay over after all and it was a long time since I'd had to think about the complex mating dance. Surely I was past playing games, but what then?

Quentin picked me up from the airport. I felt nervous and shy. In the car and recovering myself, I looked at him properly for the first time. I laughed. "You look like you've just got out of bed!"

He ruffled his hair, embarrassed, and looked at his watch. "It's only nine thirty. It was a late night." He glanced over. "Actually, I overslept. Sorry. Let's go back to my place, I'll have a shower and we can have breakfast."

We sat on his balcony drinking coffee and eating croissants. It felt like the long-ago time in Europe, and I had to blink twice to remember I was with someone new. Showered and fresh in white shorts and polo, Quentin matched the warm, clear air. He reached out and took my hand. "What do you want to do? We could take a stroll on the beach, or would you like a game of tennis?"

"I didn't bring shoes."

"There's a shop at the club."

"Okay, I'll see what I can find to wear."

He showed me a guest bedroom, laid out with a feminine touch. I wondered if he had a designer, or if someone else had lived here. I found a short skirt and a light top, changed, then messed around nervously with perfume and makeup, smoothed out the bed where I had put my bag down, and finally opened the door.

Tennis was fun. We quickly built to a surprising level of competition and I enjoyed pushing my body hard, forgetting it was exercise with my focus on points. It was close but I won. "I'm not sulking, I'm not," Quentin repeated, but not long after his grin reappeared. "What next?"

We explored the city, which I didn't know well, then spent an hour at a gallery, cool and soothing after the strong sun. I looked at the art, but in the back of my mind was the question of sex. One way or another it would have to be addressed and I didn't know what I wanted. I sat down on a leather bench, noticing my movements and posture were constrained. Quentin sat next to me and slid along so his thigh and shoulder were against mine. "Don't look so scared," he whispered. An involuntary cough of laughter escaped me. "Come on, time for a drink."

My discomfort amused him and over dinner he performed a more and more outrageous burlesque of flirtation until I cried laughing. He reminded me of the boys at school who could turn any statement, question or suggestion into innuendo. "That's it," he said, as my shoulders relaxed and I looked him in the eye. "Trust me." When we arrived back at his apartment he turned on the guestroom light and held the door open for me.

"Thanks for a great day," I said.

"No problem. Sleep well."

Now the pressure was off I lay in bed cursing myself and wondering if I should go and find him. I played a romantic sequence in my mind and it felt right, but when I thought about standing in his doorway, I was scared. What if he sent me back?

In the morning I watched him make coffee. "Sorry about last night," I said.

"That's okay."

"I feel like a fool."

"Why?"

"Because I let my nerves overcome my inclination."

He raised his eyebrows. "In that case," he said, "I was going to suggest we go out again, but perhaps you'd prefer to stay in and . . . get to know each other better."

I grinned. "Yeah, that'd be great."

39

I came back home overflowing with energy. I was booked to go back to Auckland in a fortnight, but in the meantime, I made an offer on the house on the corner and sat down to brainstorm.

Three weeks later I stood in the living room of my new venture, keys still in my hand. Doors were open wide out to the veranda and I could see trees, lawn, and the occasional car going past. I looked around, imagining how it would be, visualising the furniture, the colours, cool neutrals over this awful brown. I love this moment, when everything is possible, where I begin to create the future with my imagination.

Maria came running in. "Mum, Mum, I found a swing!"

I held out my hands. "Come here, Babe, let me tell you what I see."

Despite the frustrating Christmas break, progress was fast on the building. I had a team on the renovation and they worked together well. I asked Carl to come in and design the kitchen. He told me where to go for commercial ovens and equipment and introduced me to his wholesale suppliers – "You know you're setting up in competition with me."

"Not really, Carl." I looked at him closely to see if he really thought so. I had rarely seen him out of his chef's whites. He was tall, slightly stooped from leaning over pots and plates, with thick, black hair and stubble that was nearly half grey. The lines on his face looked somehow deeper when he was relaxed, not shouting impatient instructions and terrifying his string of assistant chefs. "How are things going at the café, by the way?"

"Oh, you know, the joys of being self-employed, scary amounts of money going out, a trickle coming in. At least I don't have time to linger in the shops, wishing for things I can't afford."

I laughed. "I'm weeping for you, Carl, weeping! How about I sweep in and rescue you? You can flag the café and work here, regular work, regular pay?"

He stiffened, offended, and I bit the sides of my mouth to stop another laugh. "Didn't think so. So it's not so bad, then?" He shrugged and I hugged him. "Don't be a stick. Let me show you around."

Simon walked down to the new place one evening with the baby in the pram. I had a box of toys Maria played with when she was tired of helping and I found a rattle, but by then Andrea was asleep. We sat on the veranda.

Simon nodded. "Well done, J."

"Thanks, it won't be too long now. It all feels right. I plan to start in about six weeks. The fliers came back today, simple, just a picture of the outside, a list of possible events, numbers, a rave about the atmosphere. I've got a list of local businesses, but I don't just want to send the information out cold. I want to talk to people, let them hear my passion for it. I know once it gets started, it will take off. There's nothing else like this."

"I'm going to a business lecture next week. Come with me if you want; there's always networking time beforehand, and you're a natural at working a room."

"Except I always come out feeling like the room has worked me. Okay, thanks."

The next day was Sunday and I went back on my own and sat on the veranda of the new building to be quiet and think.

The Power of Imaginative Creation: it was a miraculous lesson to have learned. I allowed myself a smile, then a laugh, then, looking around me at the empty room, I overlaid it with a busy scene.

A party. Who would be there? What would be happening? How would it be decorated, what food? I resisted a momentary impulse to undervalue the moment – it was easy, yes, but essential, powerful, and if I did as my impulse prompted and left now, went to meet a friend, sit in a café, this essential non-work would not be done. Where did it come from, this seductive, sabotaging urge? Worry about that later. Details now. If I could see it, it would happen.

An evening party. Lawyers. Celebrating something big – a merger? The signing of a big deal? In the guise of a fundraiser? Yes. A law firm charity fundraiser, a mild March evening, people strolling outside. Lights in the trees, gentle music, jovial chat.

Two months later, a vague hint of fresh paint disguised with scented candles and exotic food, I moved in the crowd checking everyone was happy. I caught snatches of conversation, alert for the slightest dissatisfaction so I could resolve it, but everyone was at ease, slightly celebratory in mood. I had pushed for sparkling wine to start instead of a more conservative still white wine. Even reluctant bon-vivants sang a chorus of "don't mind if I do" and "just this once" and "it's a special occasion, after all" as they hitched up their smiles a notch and prepared to be courted and charmed.

After an hour of food and drink, one of the law partners called everyone to order and began the charity auction which was the centrepiece of the evening. He was a little much one-on-one – this was where he worked best, the sole object of an audience of a hundred.

There was lots of laughter, and near hysteria as the prices wound up and up, alpha males and females locking in deadly ego battles to secure modest trophies: a mystery weekend, a hamper of food, a lawnmower, dinner with a local footballer. A huge sum was raised for a respectable charity and afterwards the evening remained charged with adrenaline which kept many dancing till two.

As I calmed the last guests and saw them to their taxis, I found a moment to acknowledge the exactness of the match, my picture to the final reality. It was an excellent launch.

Carl came out of the kitchen wiping his hands on his apron.

"Have they finally gone?"

"Hey, Carl, I thought you went hours ago, before the guests arrived."

"I came back after the café closed to sort some things out."

"You are such a darling to do this for me – I don't know where you found the time."

"Just finger food – could do it in my sleep, blindfolded with one hand behind my back, a finger up my nose and a group of wild Hungarians riding hobby horses around the kitchen."

I laughed. "Really?"

"Really, no sweat. How was it? It looked like fun."

"Wow, yeah, it was amazing. And I saw lots of people taking cards from the hall table when they left. I knew it would work, but this reality, it's better than I imagined! . . . Only . . ."

"Yeah?"

"I need to get a chef sorted. It was sweet of you today, but . . ."

"Well, let me think about it. I get more offers of talented youngsters than I can use at the café, maybe I could oversee things, train one of them – you're not thinking of sit down meals?"

"Not yet, not unless . . . well, anything could happen, my mind's open. We'll do what we can do."

"Tired?"

"There is NO way I could sleep right now."

"Maria?"

"At Simon's."

"Well, then come on. I'm not tired either. There must be somewhere in this damn town that's awake."

40

The next Sunday I arrived home from Auckland to find Nora sitting up with Simon's baby. "What's going on?" For a moment, she didn't answer. I looked at Andrea. "What?"

"Oh, God, it's awful! Ellen, she took some sleeping pills – she tried to kill herself."

I put my keys on the table and sank into a chair. "No! Poor Simon. Is she okay?"

"They're at the hospital. He phoned here – didn't you tell him you were going to Auckland? I took Maria and went to get Andrea. It was horrible. He looked dreadful. But from what he said I think she's going to be okay."

"Okay and not okay. Alive, but still a person who could do this."

"How old is Andrea? Three months, four?" I nodded. "If it's post-natal, she might just come out of it."

I blew out a fast breath. "No. No, I've been avoiding it, because I don't know what I can do to help, but this has been coming for a while. She's brilliant, Ellen, creative and warm, but there is a weak point, like a seam in marble, or a bubble in glass, which you know could make it break apart. Poor, poor Simon." I looked at the baby, asleep on the sofa. "And this little one."

We sat in silence until I finally roused myself. "You go, I'll make up a cot in my room for her. Thanks for everything."

"Sure." Nora collected her coat. "Hey, how was your weekend?"

"Great, but slightly overshadowed now."

Andrea woke early, crying to be fed. I looked in her change bag, but there were no bottles, no formula, nothing. I realised I didn't even know whether she was breast or bottle fed. Maria came out, following the noise.

"Hi, Hon. Listen, Andrea's hungry. Does Ellen give her a bottle?"

Maria looked confused. "She feeds her on her lap."

"Oh." So I'd have to find formula and teach her to drink it. I was just wondering where to start when Simon knocked and walked in. His face was white.

"Has she been crying long? They gave me this at the hospital. With all the crap in her bloodstream, Ellen couldn't feed her even if she wanted to." Implying she didn't. He pulled out a can of formula and a bottle, started to hand them to me, then tried to take Andrea. In the end he nearly dropped all three. He closed his eyes. I held Andrea with one arm and took the can from his shaking hand.

"Here, give it to me, I'll mix it up."

Simon paced with Andrea, who was now screaming. Maria sat nervously still, watching. She crept up to Simon and he put a hand on her head, but otherwise ignored her, turning to pace back again. I read the instructions on the can, sterilised and filled a bottle.

"What if she won't take it?" He shouted over the noise, tears in his eyes.

"She will, you can hear, she's hungry. Here, let me."

He watched blankly as I talked to her, stroked her head until the wails turned to whimpers, and let out a sigh as she began to drink. It took her a while to work out how to get the liquid to flow, but after that she guzzled hungrily. I stopped her after a couple of minutes to burp her. "She's drinking so fast, she'll make herself ill." Andrea's indignant annoyance brought a weak smile to Simon's face.

"Thanks, J, I was past it."

"Tell me about Ellen."

"She'll be able to come home today." He closed his eyes, a deep frown etching his forehead with lines. "I don't know what to do."

"Just be there for her, Simon, it's all you can do. She'll be okay."

"We both know that's not true. Something needs to change."

"Counselling?"

"They've recommended all sorts of things, at the hospital. Their acceptance of this as a normal state of affairs is . . . depressing."

"You know I'll help any way I can."

He nodded. "Thanks, Julia." His look was unguarded, hungry.

"You should get back to the hospital."

"Yes."

He went to take Andrea from me.

"Let me look after her today. We can stay here or go in to work if she's settled enough. Really. You need to focus on getting Ellen home."

Recovery was slow, but every improvement was a miracle. I found myself much more involved in their lives than I had been before, or really thought was wise, but it was so easy to combine babysitting Andrea with looking after Maria.

I found Ellen confiding in me in a way I thought it would be dangerous to reject. She needed to talk to someone, to trust someone. For whatever reason, she chose me, and I felt I had no choice but to go with it.

I called in often, taking Andrea out for walks, having coffee with Ellen when we returned. Ellen took an intense interest in Quentin, asking to meet him, speculating about every aspect of him, asking whether I was in love. It seemed harmless, and I was happy to take myself back to him this way. It only seemed odd that whenever Simon came in she changed the subject. There hadn't been a logical moment to tell him, and it was becoming weird.

I helped organise a cleaner to keep the house in shape and while we talked I often folded clean clothes which Ellen had taken out of the drier and not got around to sorting, or tidied toys and books into piles. I encouraged Ellen to cook, and picked up groceries, or made lists so that Simon could do it on his way home.

Simon was alarmingly grateful, and became almost as dependent on me as Ellen was. I was uncomfortable, and avoided him as much as possible at first, taking care to leave before he arrived home in the evenings. But gradually it got easier, and I came and went like part of the household.

41

Quentin was a life-saver. Seeing him was bright and fun. I didn't talk to him about the situation and while I was with him I could almost forget it myself.

I told myself I wasn't serious about him but that didn't stop the daydreams, or the nervous pressure I felt in my chest whenever we met.

He wanted to meet Maria, but for the moment I said no. She was missing her one-on-one time with Simon, and I didn't want to confuse her more.

Three months after the event, things were back to normal enough for me to confide in Quentin about Ellen's suicide attempt.

"You're amazing," he said. "I couldn't do it. I would have let them sink or swim."

We were strolling around the Viaduct after dinner, weaving in and out of groups of people enjoying their Saturday night. I turned to face him.

"Really?" The word blew a slight frost in the June night air.

"Really."

"But when people need you . . . ?"

"She's your ex-husband's wife. It's not your job."

"We were never married," and in correcting him I missed the meaning in what he had said.

"In Auckland again?" Simon asked when I collected Maria.

I took a breath. "I met someone up there. A customer, at first."

"Oh."

I went to step past him but he was staring at the ground, and didn't move out of the way.

"Is it serious?"

"No, not really."

I knew what he was thinking. I was thinking it myself. I didn't want to be tied to a relationship.

"But you've been seeing him a while?"

"It's a long distance, part-time thing. He has a business there, and I have mine here. Neither of us will move. It's not a big deal."

And that's when I realised: that was why it felt okay – there was no expectation of anything more. I relaxed, but Simon looked so sad. I put my hands on his upper arms and pulled his eyes up to mine. "Hey, Babe, you'll be fine."

He shook his head. "You have no idea."

I wandered around the office feeling lost. Nora had given me a list of calls to make to customers, just making contact, and I had looked over some design alterations which made manufacture easier, but now it seemed there was nothing to do.

"What about the Meeting House? There must be something there." I think Nora wanted me out from under her feet.

"It's booked Tuesday to Thursday for the next six weeks by a training company, and in between for a wedding, but there's an event organiser and she has her own chef, decorations, everything."

"You could be working on marketing further down the track."

"Yeah, I guess."

"Julia, I know you're bored, but just . . . look, why don't you go see Quentin. Take a few days off."

That was part of the problem. I'd lost interest there, too.

The relationship had reached a very enjoyable equilibrium. About twice a month we met for weekends while Maria was with Simon, at Quentin's apartment, my house, or hotels around the country. Maria had met him, but I kept the relationship separate from her most of the time – my ideal was that it remain very simple, a mutual engagement of equals.

But then we'd been sitting on his balcony the Sunday before last, watching gulls wheeling, echoing eerie cries. Quentin brought out breakfast and I leaned my head back to feel the sun on my face. "Wow, it's perfect here."

He grinned. "Anything to lure you to me more often. I swore I wouldn't, but I'm starting to notice when I wake up without you, starting to hate it."

"But Q, that's six out of every seven days! And you love that freedom, really."

"Sure."

I changed the subject. "What shall we do today?"

This conversation had become a standing joke. "Well, we could go to the museum, or visit my elderly aunt, or I could go into the office and do some work – you could fill in for one of the assistants, sell some furniture for me, or . . ."

"Or we could go back to bed." We both said it together, laughing. Quentin came over and took my face in both hands. "But seriously, I really am becoming addicted to you."

And suddenly something went out of it. The simple joy I felt in being with him was gone.

"What's wrong with me?"

Nora looked up again, put her paper aside and swivelled her chair around to face me. "Sit down. Tell me what's wrong. Is it Ellen?"

"Yes and no. Really it's me."

"You said she was getting better."

"That's just it, she is. And some horrible part of me doesn't like it. I'd kind of got used to being close to Simon, looking good in comparison with her. I didn't play it up, but I didn't have to: the contrast was there."

"So what are you going to do?"

"Grow up, I guess. Get over it. Behave myself."

"Can you do that? Let's face it, you're a danger when you don't have a project on."

"I know, but surely I can trust myself with him now."

42

It had been a long winter and it was a relief when spring finally arrived. I sat on the floor of Ellen's living room with Andrea on my lap, watching her flip through a board book as an exercise in dexterity. Occasionally she stopped turning pages long enough for me to point out a picture or read a word or two.

Ellen glanced up from where she was baking in the kitchen. "I don't know how you do it. She screams at me if I try to read to her."

"She's just winding you up, testing your unconditional love. Tell me about your day."

"Oh, just dull domestic stuff, nothing like as exciting as yours. I'm reading a really good book, but in twenty second bursts. Hey, and I got those photos printed, they worked out really well. Andrea looks angelic, mischievous . . . whatever . . . not a hint of the usual stubborn discontent."

I frowned slightly as Andrea laughed and pointed at the book. "Ellen, she's lovely, she's just little. Ignore her when she's horrible, all children are horrible, just to see what reaction it gets. Show me the pictures."

Ellen brought the pack over.

"These are great!" Ellen smiled and looked over my shoulder.

"That's the one I thought I'd get blown up for the hall – and that's the one to send to Simon's mother."

"Simon's mother?" I raised an eyebrow.

"Don't." Ellen bit her cheeks to stop a smile. "Don't get me started," but I caught her eye and we both burst out laughing. "Oh, shh! I know, she's mad, but Julia, not in front of Andrea."

"Coming to stay is she?" I asked innocently. "Simon said he was going to invite her."

Ellen's face fell dramatically, then her eyes narrowed. "Witch! Don't even joke about it. We're going over on Sunday to see her. . . Hey, I didn't show you what she sent for my birthday." She ran out and returned, hands behind her back, then pulled out an enormous pair of bloomers. We both shrieked with laughter.

"Just your size!"

There was a yowl from outside. I carried Andrea over to the window and saw Maria pulling Ellen's elderly cat around on a wagon. "Maria, play nice." She looked up and grinned, slowly tipping the wagon over. The cat stalked off.

"These biscuits are ready, ask if she'd like one."

"Come in and have a biscuit, tyrant!"

Ellen put the plate on the table. "Help yourself, Julia, I'll just change Andrea." Andrea screamed for a biscuit. Ellen struggled with her for a moment but then let her down. "Just one." Andrea grabbed three in her little fist and grinned like the devil, but then allowed herself to be carried out.

A key sounded in the lock and Simon came in. His eyes crinkled as he saw me, just like old times. He kissed me on the cheek. Then turned wary.

"How's Ellen today?"

"Good."

His face relaxed; he took a biscuit and ruffled Maria's hair.

"Hello, Daddy." He sat down beside her and put his arms around her.

I watched him. "You're a great dad."

He looked up and an old spark passed between us. God, be careful. Nora was right, I'm dangerous when I've got nothing to do.

"Hey, I was wondering whether Ellen would like to do some work at the Meeting House, just occasional. She's a fabulous cook, and it's just up the road. And that meeting and greeting stuff, she's great at it, that old Hostie training coming back . . ."

Simon looked worried. "Julia, I don't know, things have been . . ." He was drowned out by a scream and an awful howl. Seconds later, Andrea came running in. "Daddy, Daddy!"

He scooped her up and kissed her. "What was all that noise?"

Ellen came into the doorway, hand on her arm. "She bit me. She bit me so hard," and her face crumpled into frustrated, helpless tears.

That weekend I was supposed to be in Auckland, but I called Quentin and cancelled. "I think it's time to cool things off a little."

There was a long silence. I was determined not to break it, not to backtrack.

"A little? I'm not sure how it's possible to cool things off 'a little'."

"All right, I want to call it off. It's been great, but . . ."

"Call it off? You mean the weekend?"

"I mean us."

Another silence.

"Why?" He sounded so sad. I hadn't allowed myself to think how he'd react. The muscles beneath my eyes pulled downwards and my brow began to ache.

"I'm sorry."

"Please tell me why. It's been great. I think we've really got something."

I didn't reply.

"Babe, just come this weekend, like we planned. We can talk."

"It won't make any difference."

"Or at least say goodbye?"

I shook my head but no sound came out.

"Julia?"

"I'm sorry. I'm so sorry."

The rest of the day I couldn't be with myself. I walked, tried to read to distract myself. Nothing worked. It was a relief that night when Simon phoned. "I wasn't sure you'd be there. Listen, would it be okay if I brought Maria back early? Things are a little . . . difficult here."

"Sure. Any time you like, I'm not doing anything."

I looked around the living room, straightened cushions, stacked magazines. I felt bizarrely nervous.

Maria was nearly asleep, already in her pyjamas, so I gestured for Simon to carry her through to her room. She wriggled down under the duvet and closed her eyes. I felt a tear form and reached for Simon's hand. "I miss her so much when she's not here."

His mouth turned down and he shrugged.

"I know, my fault, my choice. But it's good to see you, too. What's up?"

He pointed back through to the living room. I stopped at the fridge to pick up a bottle of wine and held it up, a question.

"Yeah, thanks."

The liquid glugging out of the bottle seemed loud. I reached over and turned on some music, Diana Krall left from breakfast time when I was peaceful.

"I thought you might be in Auckland."

"No that's over." Another tear. I felt like an emotional yo-yo.

Simon nodded seriously, but I saw the hint of a smile. "You never quite seemed comfortable with it."

"Don't look so smug. I feel horrible."

"Who called it off? You?"

"Yeah." Change the subject. "What's happening at home?"

"Ellen's still upset. She struggles with Andrea. She takes everything so seriously."

"Did Ellen ask you to bring Maria home?"

"No, she'd never do that. But I thought Maria seemed nervous, with the tension, so she's better here."

His face creased, deep indentations in the centre of his brow. He looked old.

"Anything I can do?"

"No, I need to get back. This'll only make things worse."

I knew what he meant, spending time with me instead of hurrying back to her, but it was unguarded of him to say it.

I kissed him on the cheek as he left. "Bye, Darling."

43

With the regular travel out of my life the restlessness continued. I could start a new business, there were opportunities everywhere, but nothing grabbed my attention for more than a few minutes. Nora suggested I apply for another business award, this time for the Meeting House. I started filling out forms but my heart wasn't in it and it was slow going. Finally Nora took that over as well, put in the finishing touches and sent it away.

Maria started school and I had less to do than ever. I visited friends, took a drive in the countryside, but I felt like a ghost. The only place I felt useful was with Ellen. I had persuaded her to send a photograph to a magazine and they had accepted it.

"Hey, Ellen, congratulations, that's fantastic!" Ellen gave a little shrug. "Don't you see a different world open up? One that's not just babies and coffee mornings and all that endless feeding and changing and putting to bed, with your brain in hibernation from one day to the next? Aren't you excited?"

Ellen looked up from the cappuccino froth she was spooning to one side of the cup and back again. She smiled a sceptical smile. "Not really. You're sweet, but it's not that big a deal. It's just one picture; I've taken thousands. It's a freak event."

"But you're happy?"

"Actually I feel a bit flat. It felt good for a moment when I got the letter, but then . . . there are lots of other things to worry about."

"Ellen, why? I don't understand When are you going to be happy if not now?"

Ellen shrugged.

"Hey, you know, I read an article about this, in Cosmo, I think."

"Ever the intellectual, huh, Julia?"

I grimaced. "Don't you start, it was bad enough when Simon and I were together . . ." I stopped myself, but not in time. An awkward silence hung for a moment before I continued. "Anyway, it said that if you have negative emotions that don't fit what is happening, it can be a mistaken attempt to bring you back to a balance, a way of feeling that you think you deserve. So if something really good happens, you think of a 'yes, but.' Like, something great happens - like getting a photo into a magazine - which you have been aiming at for a long time, and then someone carves you up in traffic and that small negative thing is where you focus your thoughts; or you know you should be happy, but somehow you just aren't. You need to tell yourself you have a right to be happy, and just accept it."

Ellen pulled a wry face and shook her head. "You just don't get it, do you? It's not that simple."

I leaned forward towards Ellen and looked into her eyes. "Ellen, don't dismiss me like that, just so you can ignore what I'm saying. You are making yourself unhappy. This is great, you've worked for it. If you can't be happy now, and celebrate, then when?"

Her dissatisfaction ate at me. She had this opportunity and she was doing nothing with it. "There must be a way to make this work for you."

"I'm just not that good. If I really believed I had talent, there are all sorts of things, contributing to exhibitions, talking to shops. But I'd just be knocked back, and worse off."

"Ellen!"

She lifted both hands, turned them out and shrugged.

"Look, I know Andrea keeps you busy, physically, but what about your mind? Don't you want to have something of your own?"

At Ellen's expression I could have bitten my tongue. "Maybe I could go back to the airline."

"Look, I'm sorry, I don't mean to imply that what you do isn't enough. But you are talented."

Ellen declined to act, but I still thought about it. Then one day, an idea occurred to me. "Hey, Ellen, what if we hung your pictures at the Meeting House? With prices on?"

Ellen was doubtful. "If you like."

But the next day Simon came over.

"Julia, back off about the photographs, this isn't helping. She's not you, and she knows it."

"I was just trying to help."

"I know, J, but Ellen talks enough about not measuring up to you, and this really upsets her. I'm afraid she's heading downhill again."

"Okay, sure. Sorry." But I was left with a nasty taste in my mouth.

We got the business award and there was media interest again. With it came an offer to buy the Meeting House. I was delighted - the challenge and the creative part were over now and I was happy to move on.

Ellen seemed to sink as my profile became higher.

"You've done it again! I don't know where you find the energy."

I pulled in my cheeks. There was no answer except to play down my achievements and this was wearing thin; I was proud of myself, and tired of having to pretend I wasn't. "Ellen, I asked you to help, you could have, easily."

Ellen sighed. "I know." There was an empty silence. "Hey, but I looked out those photos you asked for. Do you still want them?"

"Great! Let me see?"

Ellen brought out a laptop and opened a folder called "Possible wall art". She flicked through them.

"Ellen, these are brilliant, as always." Ellen smiled, focused on the pictures. She seemed happiest when working with her camera, or processing the images afterwards.

"I'm sure they'll sell. How big will they blow up?"

"Pretty big. At least 100 by 80. But that's huge, you won't want them that size."

"All the better. We want people to notice."

"If you say so."

"Come down and have a look, I'll show you where we'll hang them. Then we can think about frames. If we get them up now, I'm sure the new owners will keep them."

"Thanks, but I'd better get things tidied up around here."

I looked around. About six months after the breakdown Ellen had begun to be obsessive about the house, and not a particle of dust was out of place.

"Come on, come down, have a glass of wine, let your hair down. I miss that old dry wit."

"Can we call it dry wit if it needs a glass of wine?"

I laughed. "See, there it is."

"Maybe I'll come over later."

Things got worse, tense moments became more frequent, Ellen laughed less and less until it didn't happen at all. Andrea was extremely difficult for her, but I couldn't work out why that was. She was perfect for me and only slightly stubborn when Simon had her on his own. It seemed there was a destructive chemistry between Ellen and Andrea, and they spent most of every day together alone.

"I wish I were you, she's fine for you. I'm a horrible mother."

"No, she's just winding you up. All children are worst for their parents; it's because she knows she's safe in your love."

"Do I love her?" Ellen's laugh was short and mirthless.

"Of course! You are great, you don't give yourself credit."

"No . . . look, I don't think about it all the time – usually I don't think much at all – but I have moments of clarity. I've achieved nothing. I don't even work, and look at you, what you've created, effortlessly. No wonder Simon still wishes he had you instead of me."

Oh God, she had said it out loud. "Please promise you will never think that. You are so talented, so creative! Don't expect huge achievement while you have a pre-schooler, there will be plenty of time for you to build your own career, if that's what you want, once Andrea is at school."

Ellen grimaced. "If that's what I want. Who knows? In the meantime, I'm stuck with her day after day. Sometimes I swear I see her with horns."

44

I had avoided telling Ellen about my split with Quentin, and when she found out she was bewilderingly upset. It came out in an everyday conversation, arrangements for Maria and a trip they were taking.

Ellen spun around to Simon, light arcing from her eyes. "Why didn't you tell me?"

He shrank back into his chair.

I leaned down and whispered for Maria to go check on Andrea. "See if she needs any toys."

Once I had watched Maria out of the room I turned back to Simon, waiting for his answer.

"Well?" Ellen prompted.

"I didn't really think about it."

She glared at me. "Now I know why you've been here so much lately. Well that's it." She turned back to Simon, the hate in her eyes aimed at him, also. "Send the predatory bitch home."

Soon after this there was a rapid downward spiral. Simon described coming home to a horrible scene, Ellen whimpering on the ground and Andrea standing over her with a wooden toy, threatening to "hit her again".

This time she was completely lost to us. The doctors said it would be weeks or months before she could consider coming home. Simon and I faced each other, grim practicality the only escape. "What do you want to do? Andrea can come to work with me for a while, but what about visiting Ellen, what about your work?"

"I can't think straight."

"What if I set up a bed for Andrea at my house, so that if you don't make it home by bedtime, it's easy, and she feels safe?"

"Look, I'm aware . . . I'm so grateful for all you've done, this isn't your responsibility."

"I feel so much to blame. If I hadn't nagged her about a career . . ."

"Who knows? Maybe it didn't make a difference."

"And maybe it did."

The first two weeks were hard, but once Ellen began to mend Simon was more hopeful. The girls settled into being one family, happy and stable.

One evening, when things had gone particularly well over dinner, it had seemed easier just to put Andrea into her bed in the spare room than to take her down the road in her pyjamas. We were looking at some pictures Maria had done at school, and Simon put his arm across my shoulder as he leaned in to look. I turned to him smiling, mid-sentence, and was hit with the force of my old feelings. We had not been this intimate, this relaxed, since we were together as a couple.

"Simon?" I asked, as he leaned in to kiss me; I was so filled with longing for him that I disappeared into the kiss. His hands began to move over my body and, as if emerging from deep under water, I pulled away.

"Simon . . ."

I stood, and he stood beside me, eyes glittering and primitive. "Please, just let me hold you."

I wanted him, too. He put his arms around me and pulled me close, in a tight, unmoving hug. I slowly brought my arms around him, flexed them to hold him hard and felt the tension in him build, peak, and then slowly subside. My face ached, but the moment of immediate desire was over.

"Let me explain." We still held close, he spoke into my hair.

"You don't have to."

"I could have been happy with Ellen. I never would forget my feelings for you, but I planned to make a happy life, love my children. I love her, I still love the moments with her when she is herself; I am happy to look after her, make things easy for her, but in these times when I get nothing in return, I can't make sense of it. I can make sacrifices, but sometimes it doesn't seem to do any good at all, sometimes I'm sure she would be better off without me."

"Don't convince yourself you could leave her. Nothing has changed between you and me; if we could have made it work, we would have." I pulled back and looked at him steadily.

"But Quentin, what you had with him, I think I understand now, what it was you wanted. I could do it."

"Simon, no. I know it's hard. I struggle, too, with my feelings for you. So we're being honest with each other; it feels good to acknowledge what we have pretended wasn't there. But it's not fair to her, allowing ourselves to feel this way still. It's time we did the right thing."

"I felt so sick, knowing you were with him. I'm so glad it's over."

"That's a separate issue. I can't vow chastity just because you're jealous. I have to think of you with Ellen."

"What if I said I was thinking of leaving her anyway?"

The thought was seductive and terrifying at the same time. My body wanted him, but I knew I'd only make another mess.

"No! It might kill her."

"And she might be better off without me."

"No, Simon. No."

"Hi." I leaned in the doorway of my old office, where Nora worked now.

She looked up from her desk.

"Got time for a walk?"

"What's wrong?"

"Simon."

I told her everything. "He said he's thinking of leaving her, but it would be a disaster. The only thing I can think of is to go away."

"Good idea. You should travel," she said. "The idea has occurred to me before."

"What?"

"Travel. Take some time out, just go. You're going nuts here, with not enough to do. You used to talk about the long blue horizon, time to yourself with no deadlines, no agendas."

I frowned, confused. "I don't understand."

"It's not complicated. Get on a plane. Go. Take time for yourself. A month, a year, two years, whatever."

I shook my head, resistant, but the idea had a guilty appeal.

"Can you run things without me? Or that's not what I mean to ask – I know you have been for ages. But would you mind?"

"We'll need to talk to Martin, but it'll be fine. There are some new designs to look at before you go, and later, if marketing gets slow, I'll let you know, so you can come back and work your Julia magic."

These last words echoed around my head as sounds, meaning coming as they replayed in my mind later. I was already dreaming of leaving.

"I'd have to take Maria out of school."

"So? She's five. She'll learn far more travelling. Do you want me to book flights for you?"

"No. No, I can do it. Thanks."

I sat by Ellen's bed, my hand held out to where she gripped it tightly. There was not much sign of recognition otherwise. Words ran around my head but I couldn't say anything. I wanted to apologise, I needed her absolution but I would have to do without it.

There was no sense of time passing in that room and the busyness of my life swirled to a stop. Then, with no warning, she roused herself. "Has Simon told his mother? Don't let him! I couldn't stand her triumph."

I shook myself alert. "Sheila won't be happy about this." But I wasn't sure if it were true or not, and my thoughts began to run on this course, speculating fruitlessly again on how Sheila worked, how to touch her.

When Simon arrived I let go of Ellen's hand and stepped out into the hall with him.

"You're not really going."

"I won't unless you say, I know you'll miss Maria."

He was silent, staring at the floor.

"You know it's best."

He nodded.

"I'll pick up email, you can reach us that way. And it won't be forever. I'll let you know. I'm going to see Mum in the morning, to say goodbye. Our flight's at four."

"I'll take you to the airport. Please?"

45

I sat back in my seat, tugged the seatbelt tight and looked out through the window. Travelling business class was a newly acknowledged dream, one I had always suppressed as an unnecessary extravagance, but now I hoped it would help me bring alive the joy of travel. Maria was beside me, pulling apart the entertainment pack the cabin attendant had given her. I closed my eyes and exhaled long and slow, letting the excitement and relief of the wide open space in front of me fill my body. Nowhere to be, no-one to answer to, no deadlines, no responsibilities, no projects, nothing.

I had a magazine I could read, a book, my iPod, but for now I was deep in the moment before takeoff, where anything is possible. The plane began to thunder down the runway, and then came that magical moment when the wheels left the ground, a miracle of freedom, exhilaration and perfect peace. The confusion of the last few days began to fall away.

The plane touched down at Heathrow three hours late after circling endlessly over a sea of fog. Maria was relaxed and cooperative after twenty readings of her favourite book and the fascination of the entertainment system. She had slept stretched out like a cat and woken fresh and happy.

I took our bag down from the locker, smiled at the cabin crew, then walked in real-time slow motion along the bridge and into the terminal. Thirty minutes later we were out, looking for the courtesy bus and on the way to the airport hotel where I had booked our first night. Through the scents of diesel and travel-weary bodies I picked up a smell I associated with England, indefinable.

Maria jumped on the bed, laughing, then seized the TV remote and started pushing buttons. I walked to the window and watched a plane cross the sky. I'm here. I closed my eyes and inhaled, spreading my arms wide, then bringing my hands down on top of my head. I could do anything I wanted, go anywhere I liked.

I started water flowing into the bath, took pleasure washing my hands and face; I climbed in to soak then Maria got in with me, washed herself and climbed out. I reached over to the rail and wrapped her in a towel. "I'm going to stay in for a while, okay? Can you find your pyjamas? They're in the bag."

"Okay, Mummy, I'll watch TV."

I sunk my head down under the water to drown out the unsuitable action program she selected. Silence and bliss. Once out I thought about room service but instead climbed into the huge bed. Maria snuggled in beside me.

"You okay, Darling?"

"Yes."

"Think you can sleep?"

"Yes."

I pulled her close, filled with a sense of overwhelming love. "Hold on tight, Baby, we're on an adventure."

The next thing I knew I was waking to the sunset, bright and refreshed, and wondering how to pass the night.

In the morning, following a whim, we got onto the Eurostar and in less than three hours we were in Paris.

What is it about Paris that feels like home? We walked the streets, sat in the cafés. Maria ran up and down the less popular galleries of the Louvre and a kindly guard opened the balcony door so she could sprint along the western colonnade, shouting over the sound of the traffic below. We searched the paintings for cats and spent an hour circling sculpture, Michelangelo's beautiful stone slaves capturing my attention and staying in my mind for days afterwards.

In the Musée d'Orsay I sat next to the statue of Sappho, her hands clasped around one shin, and relaxed into the coolness of the muted echoes. Maria had got used to straying near, looking around, coming back. I watched her wander, conscious of the whispered swirl of tourists eddying through the gallery, and of heavenly strength streaming silently into my soul. It was so peaceful. I had a sense of the fragmented glory of Earth and Heaven, angels singing slowly shifting harmonies on unhurried scales, in and out of tune, towards a distant but inevitable resolution.

Something and nothing led me to stand, stretch my hand out to Maria and stroll lingeringly past the statues, farewelling Sappho, pausing soon again before Cornelia and her two boys. I considered the compromise between woman and mother.

I rubbed my hand over my face and realised I was tired, my continued tour becoming purposeless before we had traversed a third of the hall. I had meant to show Maria the Impressionists but they would be there tomorrow. We looked for the exit, climbed into a taxi and returned to the hotel, exhausted, to sleep, at three in the afternoon.

Early next morning in Café Deux Magots we ate breakfast watching the loading and unloading of the goods lift down to the basement. Maria was an easy passport to acceptance by the waiters, with her dark curls and morning-plump dimples. She charmed them with her "Bonjour" and they brought her extra hot chocolate.

I wondered at the contradictions in myself. I was so far from the life I had worked so hard to create, my business, my home, but more comfortable here in the anonymity of this cool city. Maria was company, accepting, loving. I never needed to explain myself to her and I didn't feel the need for anyone else. I wrote in my journal.

I would not be anywhere else. I have so craved to be on my own, to work myself out. I look at my emotions and they pass in a parade, deep grief that is not wretched, a soaring sense of freedom, keen interest in the human interactions around me. I close my eyes and sense the beauty of the architecture – how perverse is that? If I want to experience architecture, surely I should open my eyes.

Maria began to fidget and we walked again, over bridges. She pointed to a river boat and we descended a ramp to the quai, found a Batobus stop and spent the rest of the morning cruising up and down the Seine. I had my camera and framed the city in a series of absorbable rectangles, seeing detail through the lens that I had not noticed in the wider view, and that might otherwise have passed in an undistinguished blur of light stone and tall windows.

Paris was a place to stay and we did so, day after day, week after week, strolling around the Left Bank, on the islands, back and forth to Montmartre and Sacré Coeur. After a week or so I found my French improving and got braver with the restaurants, finding that there were none where I felt out of place or unwelcome. In fact, the waiters enjoyed a single woman dining with a child, flirted and engaged me in conversation, even condescending to speak English if they saw I was struggling.

Then without warning, I knew it was time to move on.

46

The heat of Pisa hit with the force of an unexpected attack and it was some minutes before I could turn my face to the sun and celebrate it. We found the hire car and headed for the Tower, circling for a while and eventually finding a large car park enlivened by souvenir sellers and their brightly coloured goods. Maria was excited by the merchandise and we bought her a coloured jester's hat, ghastly and impractical.

It was a soft shock to move from the bustling world of airports and tourism into the detailed beauty of these buildings. Once among them they rose up huge and powerful, my gaudy fellow visitors assuming insignificance against the enormous walls of white stone. After a slow round we sat down at the base of a pillar and I took out my journal to sketch a detail, something to take away with me, and a way of experiencing that detail more intensely as my pen moved from corner to corner, curve to curve. As I drew I became calm, found things ordering themselves in my mind. What was I doing, travelling without aim? How long did I intend to stay away? I'd love to travel indefinitely, spending a week or a month in each place, getting to know it rather than endlessly passing through, as I had with Lance. But I couldn't keep Maria from Simon for too long. She was asking about him more and more now, missing him.

The little car was hot so we wound down the windows before setting out again. I followed signs for Florence, planning to take a side road before I reached it, to explore the smaller towns. It was getting late.

Volterra.

I stood on my little balcony overlooking the narrow street, the cup of coffee in my hand reminding me I was home, in a place of my own, at least for a week or two. The apartment was very plain, with terracotta floors and flat plastered walls, two narrow beds with thin mattresses, light wood dining table, a crucifix on the wall and a saint overlooking my sleep. Perfect.

I watched as an old woman in black toiled up the street below. Two children ran down, shouting, on their way to school. A few minutes later, a car appeared at the bottom, and as I watched, appalled and fascinated, it made its ascent, the driver slowing to wind down the window and pull in the wing mirror to negotiate past my building. The surprising success of this manoeuvre brought me to life and I called Maria, put the large key in my pocket and we descended the staircase to the street.

It was early and there were no tourists about yet. Shops were beginning to open, but I had no interest in buying. I looked at some crafts but mainly I wanted to see the locals living. There was a bakery, busy with people buying bread for the day. I watched from the back to see what was popular.

"Ciao, Bella!" they exclaimed to Maria as she held the door for them, touching her head and beaming up at me. My little bit of Italian was returning as I heard it spoken, and I ordered in a mixture of approximate sounds and gestures. My smile was answered by the small woman serving, my change passed with a warm "Ciao".

"Mum, let's go out!"

I knew Maria was getting restless. The apartment was small and the balcony only large enough to make a sleeping area for her doll. There was no room to run or even bounce the way she wanted to. We had found a little playground, no more than a patch of dust, really, but with a few logs placed together to look like cannons. There was a phone box near it, and every time we passed I was drawn to call Simon. I looked at my watch. It was early in the morning here. He would still be up.

Maria charged back and forth, climbing up and over the objects in an increasingly complex circuit. I stepped into the booth and tried to work out the instructions. After ten minutes of frustration I heard Simon's voice.

"Julia!"

"Hey Babe, can you call me back? My coins are running out already."

I gave him the number and waited, toe tapping, watching Maria. She was so adorable with her shouted commands to the troops and her theatrical gestures that after a few minutes I forgot to be impatient. I jumped when the phone rang, shrill and shocking. "Simon?"

"Yeah." He laughed. "How are you, where are you? Italy, I guess. It took a few tries to get through."

"I've rented a cute little flat for the week, maybe next week, too, if I decide to stay. Maria would like to talk, I'll put her on in a minute, but at the moment she's happy protecting the free world in the playground. How are you, what are you doing?"

"Good. Ellen's home, came home on Wednesday."

"That's sooner than expected?"

"Yeah." I could hear relief in his voice. "She's doing okay."

"Good."

"Are you coming back? I miss you both."

"I know. I won't stay away too long. A few more weeks. I'll get Maria."

"Wait . . ." A pause.

"Yes?"

"I'd like to be able to call you. You left your mobile, but you could get another one. Even just for emergencies?" I had a feeling he had been going to say something else.

"I need to feel . . . like I'm really away. But I'll call again, next week. Maria wants to talk now."

She had to reach up on tiptoe to get the receiver to her mouth, head tilted backwards as the cord pulled her up. I sat on a cannon and watched her face as she talked, excited and expressive, something of the Italian in her gestures already. It seemed a long time before she stopped and held the receiver out to me.

"Is Daddy still there?"

"No. He had to go. Andrea was crying."

"Ah." I felt something slip inside me.

"Are you sad, Mummy?"

"Yeah, a little. Let's go home." I took her hand and we strolled back down the narrow street, turned into the little house with its cold narrow stairs.

"I think you need a cup of coffee, Mummy."

"Yes, I think you're right."

47

Back in London in August we stayed with friends from long ago, Irish who had married before Lance and me. They loved Maria, asked about my life, and raised an eyebrow at the arrangement with Simon, whom they had met and remembered liking. I was in a mood to talk and James was always ready for a philosophical discussion on the meaning of life. Catherine was more down-to-earth, inclined to frown slightly, then laugh at the pair of us and recall James to the discussion of wallpaper for the hallway or plans for their next trip.

James was interested in my business.

"So you make furniture, buy houses, fix them up and sell them and run a meeting centre? Are you not bored with so little to do?"

I laughed. "I never meant to build an empire. And the Meeting House is sold now."

"You must have a grand life – a mansion, servants? Maria must be a real princess." James was half joking, but I knew he was curious, too.

"I try to keep life simple. We have a good local school, Maria goes there, and I'm not much of a consumer."

"And Simon, what does he do?" Catherine asked.

"He's way up in his company, management, strategic planning."

"And does he spoil Maria? Especially as he doesn't live with her full time."

I was surprised at the question. "Well, he . . . no. I guess his values are like mine. Although Andrea has whatever she asks for, I guess."

There was silence. Catherine and James glanced at each other.

"We've no children, so it's easy for us to judge," began James.

"But won't Maria be jealous of Andrea?" finished Catherine.

"Jealous?" I asked, surprised. "I don't think it would occur to her."

"But maybe in the future."

"She's more likely to pity her, rather."

"How so?"

"It's hard to describe. Ellen . . . well, I'm not the perfect mother, but Ellen is . . . not happy with herself all the time, not comfortable in her skin, you know . . ." I hadn't told them about the breakdown. Why not? James nodded, interested. ". . . and that's hard for everyone, hard for Andrea, and for Simon."

I talked more to myself. "I did what I could. It never really seemed like enough." I looked up at the expectant faces. "But that's why . . . I don't have any trouble keeping Maria's demands in check."

"And I suppose Simon wouldn't question it?" suggested James. "If he doesn't think Andrea does well from the spoiling."

I nodded. "I've never thought about it before - I suppose I forfeited my right to judge, and we could never discuss it." I remembered our last kiss, how close it came to being more. "We have been disloyal enough to Ellen."

Catherine's face was a picture of curiosity. I looked up at her and away, unexpected tears starting. "I think I'm tired from the journey. Would you mind if I went to bed?"

Next morning Maria and I left the house when Catherine and James left for work. James had recommended a walk on Piccadilly and a stop at the bookshops: Waterstones and Hatchards. We each chose books then walked down to Green Park where I read my popular psychology and Maria chased the birds. On the way back I bought a bottle of champagne and prepared again to describe my life in detail. Was it so unusual? The answer must be "yes".

After so much time without adult company I enjoyed conversation with friends, but within a few days the balance shifted. We passed a small Avis office on our way to and from the Tube station, and each time, I had a vision of a road in front of me. One morning I said a final goodbye to Catherine and James as they left for work, took ten minutes to pack our bag and pulled the door closed behind us. I felt my freedom once more as a ball of expanding outward pressure in my chest and closed my eyes, giving myself over to it as we walked to pick up the car.

The journey began as only a vague pull to the North, a wish for bleak landscapes. I thought of Yorkshire, where Lance and I had spent two days as passengers of friends who had a car back then, when we didn't. I had wanted to visit the Brontë parsonage, but the others, Lance included, had looked at me as if I were mad.

I pulled off the motorway for a coffee and to buy a better map. The name of the town, Haworth, was in my head and I found it quickly in the large-scale book. I leaned back in my chair, looking into my mind's distance, the menus and bustle disappearing. Already tired of Maria's Postman Pat tape, I bought her a portable player with headphones. The repeated rattle of Northern small-town drama mercifully silenced, I relaxed once more into the journey.

The M1 was fast and easy, mid-morning on a week day, and we made good progress towards our destination. After a couple of hours I turned off, wanting country roads and local interest rather than heading towards a distant goal. There were signs to an historic market town and we parked, strolled and booked a room for the night in a large pub which fronted onto the High Street.

Annie's Tea Shop

8th September

The waitresses are wearing the most ghastly caps and aprons, gaudy floral material. Do they do this for the tourists? But what's this, I hear an American couple behind me commenting how quaint they look, so it's maybe only cynical me who thinks the effect is overdone. Maria is charming an older woman on her own – they both look happy – so I have a few moments to think.

I'm sitting on a cushioned seat in a low window, so I can see out into the street – Marks and Spencer across the road, built into an old building which leans out over the footpath. The Laura Ashley next door is somehow more in keeping. Here in the shop, old and fake-old confuse the eye. There are aged beams and low doorways between rooms; the floor is unfakably sloped towards the back corner; but they add to this with "ye olde tea shoppe" signs, which grab the eye and twist the reading of age.

There is a woman across from me juggling a baby and a three-year-old. The food is not coming fast enough and by the time it arrives, the children will be out of sorts.

There is freedom in movement, in being a stranger. I don't need to achieve anything, do anything, no-one has any expectations of me. I'm at peace.

I lost myself staring at the people passing by, breathing deep, thoughts wandering at random. This is what I want my life to be, a series of these moments, days and weeks to think of nothing. Maria ran back and sat on her chair, talking loudly about the woman she had met. I felt a shiver of impatience as my trail of ideas vaporised. I'd have to wait now until she was asleep.

Looking out my window at the Ship Inn

9 p.m.

Strange how time passes, sometimes fast, sometimes slow. The town was bustling with commerce this afternoon, but none of the activity seemed quite directed or necessary. We stopped in at the local museum, looked at some artefacts found in local fields, a story of the colourful publican who built this inn. I have been reading "Shirley" which I bought in the W.H. Smiths. Maria is asleep now. The town has closed down, not one car in five minutes through the High Street. Time for me.

48

Having known where I was going, I felt an odd reluctance to arrive. I found myself taking insignificant side roads, finding excuses to stop. I bought art supplies, paper, pencils, colour wash, and stopped every day to sketch; to capture what I saw, but also to delay something inevitable. I looked on the map for any landmark to visit, country houses, gardens, ruins. And now a castle.

I took off my coat and lay it on top of the dry leaves, took out our sketchbooks and sat down, leaning my back against a tree. Maria had got used to the routine now. She was working on a story, Teletubbies, mostly pictures but some creatively spelled phonetic words to hold the story together. Her reading had come a long way since we left, with all the time I had to read to her. She could recite all her books anyway, and after I had read them through once she was mostly content to go through them again herself. She had begun asking "What's that word, Mummy?" and "Where does it say 'cat'?" She had learned phonetics at her pre-school and was experimenting with writing. I watched her take a green felt pen and draw a round green hill, then look for the purple for Tinky Winky. My arms fell to my sides and I relaxed.

The sky was watery blue and the afternoon sun created long, sharp shadows across the landscape and caused the remaining foliage to glow with orange and gold. I began my picture by outlining the castle, choosing to make it a silhouette rather than fill in detail. As often happened when we were sitting drawing, someone stopped nearby to watch. This time, though, rather than drifting off, the woman approached and spoke.

"I think I heard from your accent: you're from New Zealand."

I looked up, took in the soft trousers, comfortable rather than stylish, the hand-knitted jersey, the neatly permed grey hair. "Yes. You, too?"

"Yes. It's good to hear a voice from home."

"You've been away a long time?"

"Nearly three weeks. It's been very nice, seeing everything I've seen pictures of, but it's a long time." She lowered her voice to a whisper.

I looked around to see why but there was no-one near. "Sit down?"

"I don't want to disturb you."

"You're not, I can draw while we talk. Look, there's plenty of room on my coat." The woman hesitated. I reached up and offered my hand. "I'm Julia. And this is Maria."

"Margaret." She allowed herself to be guided to a seat. I went back to my picture. "My husband died . . . and my children thought a change of scene would be good for me, so they bought my ticket, paid for the tour. Very generous."

As she spoke I began to doodle around the edges of the castle, dragons and butterflies and gothic shapes. I drew storm clouds and lightning and eerie moonlight while her story dissolved into sobs.

"I'm so sorry. I never cry."

"I think it's been too much for you."

"Perhaps."

"Do you want to stop the tour now, go home?"

"That's part of it. With Bill gone, home isn't home any more. It's cold."

I felt sick, my heart filling with what I imagined was her grief. I waited while she cried, my hand on her arm, my drawing suspended. Finally her tears slowed. "Poor thing, you've lost everything. What will you do?"

She frowned. "Not everything. I have my children, my friends at work. And Bill is with me, always. Thank you, I'll be all right now I've had my little cry. I'm sorry, dear," she said, patting Maria's head. "Don't you worry about silly me."

After she had gone I felt restless, dissatisfied, annoyed. In this landscape I wanted grand emotions, unconquerable grief.

I stood up, suddenly impatient. I knew where I was going, time to go there. I gathered up our belongings and, despite a sense of foreboding, I got on the motorway. Within a couple of hours we were there.

Brontë parsonage

18th September

My heart is weighed down with the closed-in-ness of this place. I can think of Emily out roaming the moors but the house itself echoes with emptiness. Perhaps the glass cases are texturing my impressions, Charlotte's clothes preserved in stillness. I'm not getting any sense of space and wildness, I feel the suburbs closing around, like that world has vanished. I'll take another turn, try to imagine life and activity, conversation, interaction. The Brontës' static aunt burdens my impressions.

I sat on a bench and looked up at the building. There must be more to be had from this place. And I'd like to find some of that wild moorland, spend some time on it. "Maria, Honey, come with me. I need to go back in."

I went first to the shop and bought a copy of *Wuthering Heights* and Emily's poems, a dark landscape with gathering clouds on the cover. I took the book to the ticket desk, waited for a couple to pass through. Maria had found a box of toys in a corner and was taking clothes off a doll. I asked the woman at the counter about the moors. "Where do I go to see them?"

"People often ask," she answered comfortably, bright clothes and suburban hair incongruous with the mood I was seeking. "Do you have a car?"

I noted the directions and the recommendation of a pub in the wilds of nowhere – "they usually have rooms, there's nothing for miles" – then, strangely, the woman looked into my eyes. "Try the house again, dear, I think what you want to find is here." I nodded, startled and stretched my hand out to Maria.

"Don't worry, she'll be fine here for a few minutes."

This time I walked through as if I were coming in after a long walk, suspending the knowledge that if I chose, I could be anywhere in England in a few hours. I imagined being here, in this house and the surrounding area for indefinite months to come. As I did so, the walls closed in around me, the dimness became more oppressive. I imagined Charlotte's constraining dress wrapping me tight.

I looked around. Where would I write? If I couldn't travel to get away I would want to create another world with words. But then, you couldn't write sunny beaches or glittering city life while living here. This landscape would demand to be expressed; it would bring down a cloak of forgetfulness on other experience. It would be both a prison and a paradise.

49

We drove along ever-lonelier roads, winding higher, the vegetation getting thinner. We found the old pub and were given a tiny two-level room. There was a high single bed, a little cot, and on the raised area a dresser and a stone seat in the window, which looked out over rolling moorland. Mist showed up the undulations, defining the distance.

I shivered as I looked out at the damp and cold. I wondered if summer ever touched this place. Dusk was descending. We'd go out tomorrow.

19th September

I've found it. I've only walked 100 metres from the car, where Maria occupies her warm Winnie-the-Pooh world, but everything is different. Sound alternates from smothering nothing to the wind running through I don't know what. There's nothing here, so it must be the accumulation of acres of heather lifting slightly from the ground, or the distortion of the movement of the few trees I can see on the horizon. I look back towards the car but it seems a lifetime away. Imagine days and weeks of this – imagine wilder weather! At the inn they call this mild but already I'm chilled deep. Close my eyes, concentrate on this, emptiness – this is a world I want to carry inside me forever.

I opened my book, flicked through some bleak scenes in *Wuthering Heights* and read one stanza of poetry, a reference to a lost lover.

In an instant, my thoughts were with Lance, in a place I rarely while waking acknowledged I still had within me. I was faced with the choice of standing up, walking away from the emotions I had for a long time had no space for, shutting them down again; or taking the opportunity, allowing them to wash through me and experience them, bleak as they were, to the full.

My thoughts returned to Lance that night. I was confused by it, not sure whether to welcome the change or reject it. It was so long ago, nine years, but still, I realised, such a central part of me. I was reliving my feelings for him, my time with him, as if no time had passed in between. In the dark of the chill room I felt as if I could reach out and touch him, and he became even more vivid in my dreams.

Is this what I was looking for? I asked myself, slipping in and out of sleep.

"God, I hated seeing you with Simon." Was the voice in my head? It seemed so real, so immediate.

"I know. I knew you would. Even in London you always seemed jealous when I talked to him."

"I knew he wanted you. And I knew you fancied him."

"But I didn't."

"You thought you didn't, but you did. I wanted to get rid of him so I told him every time I fucked you, when and where, and what we'd done."

"No! No wonder he stopped coming to see us."

"It was such a relief. I think I could have seen you with anyone more easily than with him."

"But why?"

"Because I knew he'd be better for you than me. He would give you what I couldn't."

"Fidelity."

"Ah! You knew. And I thought I was so clever. Why did you put up with it?"

"It was part of the package, part of you. But I often wonder what our life would have been like. Right about now, for example, would you be on your third 22-year-old wife, or would it have been a series of affairs?"

"So you're glad I didn't stick around."

Tears formed in my closed eyes and rolled over the pillow. "No. I wanted you to stay, forever."

"And why? You were better off with Simon, you know you were."

"Not better off, it was just different. And I couldn't make that work, either."

"You know, I'm glad of it, not to see you with him any more. But really, if I ever tried to get my head around it, I don't know what you were afraid of with him."

"I wanted to build my own life, I needed to know I could look after myself."

"No, that's not it. That's what you told Simon, but it wasn't the truth."

"It was."

"It wasn't. I could see, I could always read you better than he could, even if I didn't seem to care. That wasn't the truth. So what was it?"

"Oh, SHIT! All right! It was because I knew you wouldn't like it. I was being faithful to you. Whenever I focused absolutely on Simon, began to really fall in love, I felt you there, hurting, angry, jealous. So I held back. I didn't want to let you go."

"Hah!" he laughed. "So it worked. I thought you could feel when I was there. I ruined your happiness from beyond the grave. Both of you. Deliberately. Ironic, considering I would have said, as far as I loved anyone, that it was the two of you."

"I think I want you to leave me alone now."

"You think?" he taunted. "Not sure? Wouldn't you miss me if I were finally gone? Are you sure this isn't your imagination after all?"

"Fuck off and let me go to sleep."

The feeling of being shadowed by Lance continued. It was like walking through a dream world. I felt distant in my interactions with ordinary people, and found myself avoiding them whenever I could. There were no more half-dreamed conversations but I was drawn into a seductive feeling of being near him and I didn't want to leave it behind. Even with Maria I felt separate, like I was wrapped in cotton wool.

Days turned into weeks and we stayed in the lonely inn on the moor. The landlord's daughter loved to babysit, so I took long walks, coming back to eat dinner and wonder what I had thought about all day. Not about the future or the present, nor even really about Lance, although I became more and more convinced that his presence was real rather than imagined. It was as if I were under a spell, slowly being drawn from the world of the living into the world of the dead. Emily's description of Heathcliff so closely matched my experience that I wondered whether she had known something similar, too.

"Julia, how are you?"

"Nora. How wonderful to hear your voice!"

"We haven't heard from you in a while."

I was puzzled; surely it hadn't been longer than usual.

"How are you? Everything going okay?"

"Everything's fine. I just wanted to check up on you. You haven't been answering my emails."

"Really?"

"Any idea when you'll be back?"

"I'm not planning ahead much at the moment. Maybe the end of September."

"It's already October."

I frowned. I felt an uncomfortable pull back to my old life. "Well, then. Soon. I'll come home soon."

I hung up and blinked twice, as if waking, then began a slow climb out of the strange land I had been inhabiting. "Where am I, who am I, and what am I doing?"

50

I must think about getting home. My head felt fuzzy, as if I was still half asleep. Email. How long was it since I had checked? How could it be October? I asked the landlord, who thought there was an Internet café in a town ten miles away.

"Thanks, I'll go tomorrow."

That night, my dreams were stranger than ever. Lance's voice sounded from all sides of the room, echoing and booming, but I couldn't make out the words.

I drove to the town; after the still of the moor the small High Street seemed busy. I looked in one or two shops and asked for the café. I was directed into a little side alley, with grey buildings closing over me. I ordered a sandwich and a biscuit and got out a colouring book for Maria, then opened my email. Four messages from Simon and three from Nora. The oldest was three weeks old. Could it have been that long since I looked? Not concentrating well, I simply repeated to each what I had said to Nora last night. I would be home soon. Ellen's message, however, shocked me into focus. It had been sent just the day before.

I so wish you were here. I can't manage Andrea at all. Since I got back from hospital things are worse than ever, like she's testing me. Simon says not to worry, but she's different when he's here, he doesn't see it. She wouldn't treat me like this if I were a better mother, if I were you. Will you look after her, Julia, if anything happens to me?

I sat completely still. This was not like Ellen's other cries for help, hints of suicide, this was more internal, and more final, setting things up for after she was gone. I closed my eyes but instead of a vision of Ellen, all I got was the taste of Simon's kiss. Dread and guilt flooded in and my mind spun with different views of their relationship, how I had made things worse, how Ellen certainly would have been more confident with Simon if I hadn't been around. But how could I have done anything differently? Maria, Ellen, Andrea, we all needed Simon. I closed my eyes again. I should have kept my feelings for him under better control. How much does she know?

"Hold on, Ellen, wait, I'll come," I wrote, and went back to the inn.

I booked seats on the next day's flight and spent a last restless night in Yorkshire. Towards dawn, as I was sleeping, Lance's voice came again.

"Go back to Bruges."

"I can't go back to Bruges. I'm going home."

"Please."

"Lance, I can't, I have to go home."

The flight came into Auckland early but at seven I thought Ellen would be up. Simon's voice answered, raw and croaky. "Hello?"

"Simon, it's me."

"Julia! Where are you?"

"I got an email from Ellen, I was worried, is she there?"

There was a long pause. "No, she's not." A dreadful silence followed. "Where are you? I hate to . . . can you come?"

"I'm in Auckland, I'll be there in a couple of hours."

51

I fought with guilt. It was horribly strong and it knocked me off balance. I sat in Ellen's kitchen, feeling cold. Andrea was quiet and unnaturally still, uncharacteristically accepting of Maria sitting asleep on Simon's knee. Simon spoke little and I had trouble meeting his eye. The mood was dark, and neither of us knew how to deal with any of it.

Nora came to take Maria.

"Hi, Hon, are you okay?"

"I'll get over it." I spoke as shortly as possible, I couldn't bear the sound of my voice.

"When's the funeral?"

"Thursday."

She blew out a breath and reached out her hand to Maria. "Hi, Darling, welcome home. I'll take you back to your place." She looked up at me. "Do you want me to take Andrea, too? It's late and she might sleep better away from here."

I looked at Simon for an answer. He nodded.

"Thanks."

The door closed and a stone stillness descended. I walked back to the dining table and sat down. Simon stared at the table top, hands in his lap. I so wanted to help him. The ice in my chest began to thaw.

"Why do all my women leave me?"

His question hung in the air. Finally I reached down to take his hand and led him to the sofa.

He sat and slowly turned his face towards me. "Why?"

"We adore you, we're just fucked up."

Tears appeared in his eyes and I put my arms around him and pulled him close. He relaxed into my embrace and let his tears fall; I kissed his cheek and found I was crying myself. I thought we could cry out everything inside us, but Simon turned his head so my next kiss landed on his mouth and within seconds an enormous need for him burst open. I wanted him so badly. It took all my strength to stand up from the sofa and take myself home.

I was still on UK time and the hours ticked slowly by. I cooked omelette and toast, wide awake till four a.m. I found there was hatred for Ellen within my guilt and confusion, and the strongest desire for Simon infused with lust for revenge. She had kept him from me, and she had hated and envied me.

When I finally slept I dreamed vivid dreams, of making love with Simon then of Ellen, screeching, and when I scorned her, Lance's grave and my promise.

His voice rang like crystal. "You said you'd never love anyone else!"

"But you didn't stay!"

I woke and felt my heart thumping. Nora appeared at the doorway.

"What is it? You called out."

"Thank God, thank God it was a dream."

I must have been possessed. Every face around me at the funeral was strained and deeply grieving. How could I have envied Ellen? I knew what she went through, at times I had been the only one she confided in; I knew how she struggled. In the light of day my compassion for her returned.

There were mothers from Andrea's pre-school, elegant men and women from the airline, Ellen's parents, stunned and silent; in their presence I felt my own grief. I would miss her, too. Even Sheila was crying. Would she have cried for me?

I saw Simon's turmoil as speaker after speaker talked about his loyalty and love. Andrea clung to his neck as he stared at nothing. I tried unsuccessfully to catch his eye. Only I knew what was going through his mind. People praised me, marvelled at the generosity of my relationship with Ellen. Moment after moment I was afraid I would jump up and confess.

Afterwards I busied myself handing around tea, moving quickly to keep out of the way of everybody's kind words.

Maria settled back into school. Simon talked about finding a day-care centre for Andrea but it made sense for her to be looked after at the factory. He had no will to argue.

I went back to work but my heart wasn't in it. Nora directed and helped me as far as she could. She took me home for dinner with her and Martin.

"You need something new to focus on. What do you want to do?"

"I need to make a difference, do something generous. An idea has been brewing, a new business venture, but one that would help others, too. Can I tell you?"

"Sure. Go on."

"You know I've been thinking for a long time abut a small hotel, since we did that bed and breakfast in Queenstown. While I had the Meeting House it seemed a good idea, it would bring in more business from outside the city. But that's not quite it. I want a project with more heart. I've thought about a living complex, just for single parents. Some of our workers could use it, and other people as well. What do you think?"

I waited nervously. Would they think I was mad? They exchanged a glance. Martin spoke first. "Tell us how it would work."

I warmed up as I talked about it. I could see it so clearly in my mind. "I love the idea of making life easier for people. It would be a community, designed with their specific needs in mind - affordable, but with heart. There would be a play area, a communal laundry, and it would a safe environment for children - I'm thinking we'd keep the garages at the entrance, so there would be no cars driving through . . . you don't want to hear all the details, but they're clear in my mind."

"And is it a business venture, or a charity?"

"Charity, I guess. But it has to be practical. It has to work in the long term."

Later, Martin disappeared into his office to let us talk.

I watched him close the door and turned back to Nora. "You know, I'm almost jealous of you two, this thing you have."

"What exactly do you think it is?"

"I don't know . . . Trust, security. And love."

"That pretty much sums it up."

"I wish I could have it, too."

"You can. You just have to want it."

"Hmm. You make it sound so easy."

"Julia, it really is."

52

The project was exciting. As usual when I was starting something new, it occupied my thoughts and conversation to the exclusion of everything else.

I drew up floor plans, with details that maximised use of resources at the same time as being fun for children: bunks over storage areas and desks, dining tables that folded out from walls, built-in furniture in a small area for watching television. The units varied in size, from a tiny two-bedroom for a parent with one or two young children, to a larger one that would accommodate up to five.

It made sense to build it near the factory, so any of the workers who wished to live there would be near work. There was a modest, pleasant suburban area five minutes' walk away, and I focused my search for land here.

"We need quite a lot of space, for garages, play area, as many units as we've been talking about. But I know there will be something, we just need to look with an open mind."

I was leaving it till the last minute to involve the architect, wanting the chance to exercise my imagination without constraint. There was no rush, although my enthusiasm told me otherwise, and everything was flexible, from the number of people it would house, to the final arrangement of buildings.

I took a walk around the area every day, sometimes on my own, sometimes with others. Nora knew what I was thinking about, and looked for possibilities with me.

Once we had the draft plans I got more specific. "We either need three of the normal-sized sections, or something unusual. And they had better be old houses so we can just pay land value."

Nora called me a day or two later. "I got the area plan from the council. It's amazing, what's tucked away in here. Come and have a look."

She pointed out three large sections back from the street. "Let's walk past these today, see if we can work out what's there."

I pulled on my coat.

"I didn't mean now, at lunchtime."

I rolled my eyes. "Nora, come on!"

One of the properties was hidden down a tree-lined drive. We had walked past before and wondered what was there. "Come on." Nora nervously followed me to a gate at the point the drive ended and the section opened out.

I gaped. "Wow."

Nora whistled. "Who would have thought anyone was living like this here?" The house was ivy-covered red brick with tailored lawns, box hedging and an octagonal summer house.

"Guess this one's out."

"Yes."

"Okay, so where next?"

The next place looked like a possibility, the house built on one corner and much of the land an overgrown vegetable garden.

"I'll go and ask."

"Just like that?"

"Why not? The worst they can do is say no. What else do you suggest?"

An old woman came to the door, thin and neat in a floral dress and apron. She was uncertain at first, but soon warmed to us. I explained the project, what we wanted to do and why. "I'm not asking you to sell to us, but just whether you might be thinking of selling any time soon."

"It sounds interesting. Come in and have a cup of tea."

We stepped into the dark interior of the hall. The smell was damp and stale, the windows half-covered with heavy curtains.

We sat in the kitchen which was clean and tidy and looked out into the back garden, where an old swing hung from a tree.

"I'm Clara. Albert, my husband, he looks after the vegetables, they are the pride of his life. So you understand, I can't sell the land to you."

Nora made ready to leave but I settled in for more conversation.

"Is Albert home?"

"No, dear, he's in the hospital, but I'm hoping every day they'll say he can come home. So you see, I can't sell his garden when he'll be back any time, wanting to work in it. It's a lot of work, but he loves seeing the results, vegetables like you can't buy in the shops any more, with such flavour, ugly looking things like they used to be, but who sees that once they're cooked?"

"Does he sell them?"

"Oh, no. He gives them away, to our children, and their friends, and to the old people's home around the way, and to the church people. I'm sure they're missing them while he's away, and I worry about the garden, but he says, no, it's good to let the ground rest, let the growth go back into it, it will just be better when he starts up again."

"You must miss him."

"Yes, but I take the bus in to see him twice a week, and we do laugh when we are together, the nurses have to quiet us . . ." She paused, happy and sad at the same time. "And you have a furniture factory, aren't you clever! And it sounds very good, what you want to do, I worry about the young ones now, with houses so dear, and so many fathers running off like they never did when we were young."

I nodded. "I'm so fortunate, and grateful. I want to use some of what I have to help people. And I'm sure we'll find the right place."

We walked down the drive in silence, not speaking till we got back to the road. "Great house," I remarked.

"What? It was awful."

"I know, it was dingy and not well looked after, but you saw how she struggled even to make the tea, I bet it was better kept when she could manage it; and all the original features are there. It's not a big house, but it has a vivid soul."

"Anyway, we're no further on."

"But we made that woman's day! I bet she hasn't had visitors in weeks. These children seem happy to take the vegetables, but did you notice she didn't mention them apart from that? I must make a point of visiting now and then."

We looked at the third property, but it was on a unit title, nine ugly 1970s flats each owned separately with a share of the land. It would be nearly impossible to arrange to buy all of them. "We'll keep looking. The right thing will come up."

53

The evenings were still strange. Most days I took Andrea with me when I collected Maria from school, then Simon would collect her after work, at six or seven, sometimes eight. He seemed to be working longer than before.

"I got behind over the last few weeks," was his explanation at the beginning, but his days were getting longer rather than settling back to the old routine. I felt awkward with him, and wondered if he felt the same way. Then sometimes it would be like old times, I'd be cooking when he came in and offer him dinner, he'd eat and play with the girls and leave happy. It was all very confusing.

Needing more to keep me fully occupied, I began a project at home, also. Maria's room was small and Andrea often slept in the spare room – plans for a small addition became a major rework. If we went up instead of out, we could fit in a pool without losing too much lawn. At the same time a neighbour's house came up for sale and I bought it.

"The land is worth far more than the house, I'll rent it for a while, then use it for a tennis court once we've paid for the extension."

In the final design, I got a suite upstairs: bedroom, bathroom, small sitting room with balcony; Maria would take over my downstairs bedroom and her room would become a games room. When Andrea stayed she was happy in the little bedroom and since her mother's death she had become resistant to change, so we wouldn't move her.

As a plan to keep busy, this one backfired – with the building going on I could no longer think or work at home. I went to the factory and begged Nora for something to do. "Hammering, painting, anything."

"Not today, thanks."

"Well, can I at least, I don't know, answer the phones? Anything."

"God, Julia, okay! But sit over there, don't distract me. I need to concentrate."

I swivelled on the chair she pointed out, looking around the office. It had an air of well-organised industry, boards full of current projects, time-lines and work rosters. Everything Nora needed to know for the efficient running of the business was on display, accessible. And everything she didn't need to hand right this minute was out of view – this had been my downfall, stuff everywhere, current mixed with out-of-date. I spun around again, relieved when the phone rang. The last thing I needed was a reminder of my inadequacies.

It was Clara. "Hello! How are you?"

"I'm fine, my dear, fine. I wondered if you might have time to come and visit."

"Of course. I'll be right there."

"I didn't mean now, Dear, I know how busy you are."

"It's fine. I'm free. I'll see you soon."

Nora raised her eyebrows. "You're leaving?"

"That was Clara."

"What did she want?"

"Just a visit. I think she's lonely." I shrugged. "See you soon."

"So nice of you to come, my dear, so kind. I did want to talk to you, and the sooner the better."

We sat over tea and Clara said she had spoken to Albert about me. "He was interested, said how nice I'd met you. Then he was quiet for the longest time, and told me he didn't think he would be able to manage the garden any more, even when he did come home. He asked me to bring you in to meet him."

"Shall we go now? I could go back for the car."

"Tomorrow will be fine, if you have time. Let's just talk now. You look tired, and worried. What is it?"

"Nothing new. Really, I'd rather talk about something else. What have you been up to?"

The next day I picked Clara up and we went to the hospital. Albert was frail but his eyes were warm and alive.

"We want to sell you our land."

I hesitated. "I don't know how to react."

"I like the idea of what you want to do. It's like me, in a way, with my vegetables, making people's lives better, easier. I can't carry that on any more, and it makes me sad. I would like the land to be used to help people, even if it's in a different way."

"But you'll go home to the house. It's your home."

"Yes, leave the house there, we'd like to live in it while we can, but I don't mind looking out at children playing instead of a garden I can't look after properly."

I turned to Clara. She nodded. "Yes. I agree. Leave the house for us while we're alive, but you can work around us, I'm sure. We'll love the company, and the idea of helping."

"You don't want to discuss this with your children?"

Albert's face was firm. "No, we can make the decision without bothering them."

"Well, we'll show you what we plan to do, and if you like it, then thank you, I'm delighted!"

54

There was something powerful in Albert's frail handshake and warm gaze. The feeling of him stayed with me after we left him.

"I don't find many people to look up to, but Albert is something special," I said to Clara on the drive back.

Her eyes sparked with amusement. "Oh yes, he has an effect on the ladies. I can't wait until he comes home."

I reached my hand out to hers. "I bet."

I took Maria back after school to look at the property again. Clara called her "Dear" and patted her black curls. "What a beautiful child!" I laughed: usually Maria ducked away when she was petted, but she drew closer to Clara and looked up at her.

"Can I go on the swing?"

"Of course, Dear."

"It's wonderful, so much more than we'd hoped! We can have a real garden, with a lawn for kicking a ball around, and some space for riding bikes."

Clara nodded. "I can just see it."

I hesitated, wondering how to approach the next topic tactfully. "I'd like to do something for your house, as well. You've not had any help with it for a long time, there must be some things you'd like done?"

Clara looked into my face, and for a moment it seemed she would be offended. "Of course, you are right. Since the children left we live mostly in the kitchen, the rest has got a bit tired."

"I have a team of people – painters, builders. It would be so easy to do whatever you want."

"Thank you, Dear. I would like the drawing room to look better than it does. My mother always kept hers perfect."

As well as my own funds we had investment from a philanthropic property developer, a friend of Martin's. He had contacts in the council who helped us get agreement for what we planned to do. I hoped it wouldn't be long before we could start. I visited often, showing Clara the plans, giving her updates on progress. Nora and I took turns to drive her to see Albert, whom we usually found sitting up in bed peering at the plans, and coming up with suggestions and improvements.

"He's so much better," said Clara. "This has given him an interest, without so much weight of responsibility. I see him stronger every day, and when he talks of being home, there's so much longing in it, he's making himself get better."

I hoped he wouldn't be ready before the heavy work was done. Albert needed lots of rest, and bulldozers and pile drivers wouldn't help him. But I didn't say anything; let him make his own decisions.

In fact, he arrived home the day the building started. He loved being amongst it, hobbling with his cane along the strips of newly laid foundation, gesturing to anyone who would listen to his vision of the future.

I stood with Clara one day, watching him. "You know, you and Albert have become like parents to me."

Clara turned to me. "We were wondering, what about your own parents? You never talk about them."

"No. What can I say? It's complicated. I don't really understand either of them. My mother lives in Ashburton. I left home when I was seventeen, I go back now and then, but we don't have much in common. I think that's why I am so in love with Maria, it's a chance to create the perfect mother-child relationship, to recover what I missed out on. She makes it easier with Mum, too, something to talk about."

"What about your father?"

"He's a free spirit. Disappeared into the ether when I was about twelve, but he'd come and gone so much, no-one really noticed exactly when it was he didn't come back." Why didn't I tell her the truth, that he'd tried to see me, and I'd refused? That even now he contacted me almost every week asking to see me, and I made every excuse I could think of? I felt a surge of guilt as I thought what Maria was missing because of my stubbornness.

"Well, I think Albert really thinks of you as a daughter. We are very happy to have found you."

"Albert and I have a lot in common."

Clara's eyes twinkled. "Yes, you do." She hesitated. "What about Maria's father? You're not together?"

I took a deep breath through my nose. "It's complicated. We're friends, still. I see a lot of him."

"And?"

"And what?"

"It just sounded like you were going to say more."

"Did it? I think there is more, I'm just not sure what."

Like the family-friendly factory, the housing complex drew a lot of attention. Only single parent families would live there, and the rent would be low. There was a covenant on the property that it always be run this way, and Albert and Clara had accepted a modest price for the land on this basis. The building would be closely controlled to keep costs down, but with some of the extra features Albert and I had thought of adding character and fun. The playground equipment was being subsidised by the manufacturer. I persuaded them it would be good publicity once the project became known, and Lisa from the factory was a wiz with plants, she had teams of parents organised to plant out the gardens once the time came.

We had created a charitable trust to own and run it.

Again the newspapers came, and this time the television news took an interest. People suggested creating similar complexes in other cities and asked for advice.

Sophia, the photographer from House and Garden, had been sent by one of the other magazines she freelanced for to do a feature. We sat talking after we had finished our interview. "So this keeps you busy?"

"My part is almost done now. I come in every day to check on progress, but that's really the architect's job. I get in the way more than anything."

"And business then, that's where you spend your time."

"No. Nora runs the business. I'm the ideas, the energy, but once things are running, I get bored. I'm consulting on other housing complexes, but that's just repetition now, too."

"So what next? I know you, you're a whirlwind, never still for long."

"I don't know. It's a blank." A familiar impatience overtook me, it was all I could do to stay in my chair. My cheeks dragged down.

"So then . . . And what about love?"

I recoiled. "Why do you ask?"

"Just curious. Didn't mean to offend."

"Oh, I'm so confused! I make such a mess of things, it seems pointless beginning. I'm a jinx, a curse, a catastrophe."

Sophia nodded slowly, eyebrows raised. "So then. No love."

55

Maria had begun to ask why Simon and I didn't live together. She looked around at her classmates and realised not everyone lived like us. One afternoon she tried a different approach.

"Mum, you're not fair to Dad."

"What do you mean?"

"Well, you let Andrea stay the night, but not him."

"Sometimes it works out easier for Andrea to stay, if she's been here, or if she wants to – you know what she's like. Sometimes it's easier to do things her way."

Maria frowned.

"I'm not saying you should misbehave to get what you want," I added, quickly. "You're very good at asking for things nicely."

"But what about Dad? He'd like to stay, and you never let him."

"What makes you think he'd like to stay?"

"Mum!" She rolled her eyes. "I look at his face."

"Well, that's not . . ."

"And I asked him," she said, with finality. "He said, 'Yes'."

For Maria's sake, I finally consented to see my dad. He stood in the doorway and lifted her off her feet, holding her high in the air in a way that took me back to my own childhood. I felt like I was flying and had to steady myself against the coffee table. She laughed, my own high-pitched giggle. She was charmed, just like every woman in the world.

"Dad, sit down, have tea."

He demurred.

"Or coffee?"

"Yes, coffee!" Maria clapped her hands. "Mum's got such a cool new machine!"

"Coffee then. Thank you. White, no sugar."

He sat on the edge of the sofa as I stepped into the kitchen and turned on the machine. I took my time frothing the milk, although he hadn't asked for it heated. Maria kept up a chain of conversation, but in the gaps as she ran to and fro fetching things to show him, I felt his eyes on me.

"What is it, Darling? What could have gone so wrong?"

"What do you mean?" I looked up in genuine surprise.

"You're dead behind your eyes."

My nose twitched. "Can't I be angry? Can't you accept my anger, after all these years?"

"I don't mind your being angry with me, but that isn't it. That's not what I see. You've gone. Gone completely."

I pulled my lips forward, generating some anger now.

"Six years you've been asking to see us, and now this is what you say to me."

"It's none of my business."

"It's not that. I don't really care what's your business. It's just not true."

276

We stared into each other's eyes now for a long twenty seconds. Maria came back into the room but still he held my gaze. I found it remarkably easy to lie, to deny what he said. Thinks he knows me. He knows nothing.

Finally, he gave a short nod. "Accept my apology. My mistake." The movement of his eyebrow was sceptical, but he covered it quickly. I brought over the coffee. Maria begged a biscuit for him.

I felt a little guilty. "Show Grandad your maths book, Sweetie. He's really good at maths, just like you."

It was coming at me from all sides. The final straw was when Quentin turned up, unannounced, and dragged me out to a restaurant. I had almost lost the will to live, or he never would have got me there.

I kept my eyes from his face. "Come on, Julia. What is it? Where are you? Look at me. What went wrong?"

"It just got too serious. I told you, I didn't want serious."

"But why? Why not? We're great together."

"I know. I know!"

"So if not with me, with who? Is it Simon? Nora told me about his wife."

"See, there you go. I'm the kiss of death."

"Don't be ridiculous. You did more for her than anyone."

"Shut up! I can't stand it when people say that. I don't need it coming from you."

"Are you saying you honestly think it was your fault?"

"Does that surprise you?"

"Of course it bloody does. I don't know what I expected, but it wasn't

277

this. Who else have you told?"

"No-one. They couldn't help."

"Well, someone needs to shake you out of it. What are you going to do? Keep yourself aloof and separate your whole life?"

"Why not? It's safer that way."

"For who?"

"For me. For everyone."

"Sounds like you should take Ellen's way out."

"How dare you! I'm here, for Maria. I'm not a coward."

"See there. So she was a coward. So it's not all your fault."

"Shut up! Talk about something else or I'm leaving."

"Some role model, though, for your daughter."

"What do you mean?"

"A mother who doesn't love. How 'bout that?"

"I do . . . I'm not . . . Leave me alone. You knew, you knew this about me. I said I wanted to keep it light. You're such a bastard."

"And you knew that about me. That's how you like us, isn't it, your men? Is that what was wrong with Simon, that he wasn't a bastard?"

"Shut up! I really can't take it." Tears were streaming down my cheeks now. Quentin's face became sober, rueful. "Take me home?"

"No, Darling. It's okay. I'm sorry. I just needed to get through. You're so . . ."

"What? I'm so what? More abuse."

"You're so separate. I just needed, just once, to see the real you." He came around the table and wrapped his arms around me. I closed my eyes so I wouldn't see other people staring. I clung to him, just managing to swallow the sobs that were rising.

Somehow I recovered enough to stay for the meal. Perhaps I needed a good cry, the food tasted better than I remembered experiencing in a long time.

He dropped me home. The light was on, but I knew Maria was with Simon, back at his place.

"Am I coming in, for old times' sake?"

I shook my head. "No."

"And are there going to be any new times, for us?"

I looked into his eyes. He pressed his lips together, opened his mouth to say something, then kissed me on the cheek and turned away.

56

I waited on the shore at Sumner for Nora to arrive. The air was cool and I turned into the breeze to inhale. My head spun with the details of the last few months, since Ellen died and I began my attempt to redeem myself with good works. I couldn't make it make sense.

"Julia!" I turned and smiled at Nora's welcoming face. Her hair, still long, still almost black, was flying in the wind. From a distance, in her jeans and jumper, she looked like a teenager still. I hugged her and found myself crying with relief.

"Hey, hey, Hon, it's okay. What is it? Come sit down."

"I'm just emotional. No, let's walk."

We went first around the sandy beach, walking out to the water then along, footsteps crossing as we anticipated each wave. I took off my shoes and rolled my jeans up, pulling my coat in tightly to stop it flapping.

"Julia! It's freezing!"

I gave her our old dare gesture. "Still afraid of the water?" and Nora laughed and prepared to wade as well.

"Thanks for coming, I needed to see you away from the office . . ."

"So? What is it?"

"Everybody keeps saying that I'm cold and distant. But I'm still me right? I'm still me."

She was silent.

"Nora, what?"

"You've been different, since . . ."

I glared at her, daring her to continue.

"What's happening, with you and Simon?"

"Nothing."

"Why not?"

"Now you, too!"

"Who else. Simon?"

"No. He's got more sense. Quentin. And Dad."

Nora laughed.

"It's not funny."

"You don't see the irony, of your jilted lover telling you this? Why would he make it up? Where's the motivation?"

I glared harder. "This isn't what I brought you here to talk about."

"Well, okay. We'll get to that. Don't change the subject, though, not again."

"Again?" But I knew what she meant, she had tried to talk to me about this many, many times.

"What's in the way?"

At that moment, I felt it all fall away. The pretence, my strength, everything that was holding me together. "Ellen. And Lance."

There was a moment's pause. We had never spoken about Lance. I hardly knew how I did it but I kept a force-field around the subject, no-one ever approached it. Except Sheila, whenever she could get near enough for a knife-thrust.

"Tell me about Lance."

I stepped out of the water and sat to put my shoes back on. The wet sand made my sock drag as I pulled it over my foot.

I smiled, but a weight pulled down inside my chest. "Lance was handsome and funny and clever. And a little bit cruel. He liked to play with people." I took a deep breath, and took myself back to the beginning. "We met in London – it was Simon who introduced us. Lance was a lawyer, two years older, he'd been working there for a couple of years. When I met Lance, I loved him instantly. The boys at university were always a little bit in awe, but Lance never treated me with kid gloves. He understood me."

Nora sat down next to me. "Go on."

"There's not much more to tell. I loved him, we got married, he died. And it hurt so much, I didn't want to risk it happening again."

"There's more – something more with Simon. That night you told us about Lance, Simon was angry. I've never seen him angry, any other time."

"Lance knew Simon liked me. And that I loved talking to him. He was jealous. So he put a wedge in, stopped inviting him over. He told me he'd curse Simon if I ever let him touch me. Wow. I'd forgotten that."

"And you believed it?"

"No, I'd forgotten it, I said."

"Well, he sounds like a nice piece of work."

"It sounds worse than it was."

There was a cool silence. After a minute Nora put an arm around me. "What about Ellen?"

"I feel awful. Maybe it was my fault. If I'm honest, I envied her . . ."

"Surprise, surprise!"

I pushed Nora away but kept on talking. ". . . maybe I was partly responsible for her unhappiness, for her death – always being there, a contrast, everything she wished she was, and making sure Simon saw it."

"Maybe you were."

"Nora?"

"You'll feel better if you face it. You're so busy trying to prove to yourself and everyone else that you're perfect that you screw things up and you don't know why. Wouldn't it be a relief to admit to yourself you're a bitch sometimes, and then get on with enjoying your life?"

I felt like I'd been punched in the chest. Every part of my body wanted to jump up and run, but I was mesmerised by her words and they sank deeper and deeper. "You're right. Why don't you hate me?"

"I guess I do sometimes, but I'm no better, none of us are." She stood up and turned to walk up the beach again. I followed.

A few minutes passed. I pulled my hair back off my face. "When I first saw Simon with Ellen I was so jealous I wanted to scream. I've never had that reaction with anyone else. I'd see Lance look at other women, and that was just him. But Simon is faithful, so I knew I had given him up absolutely."

Nora pulled her jumper tight around her and turned her back to a stronger blast of wind. "Well, it turns out you hadn't. What does he want?"

I shrugged, turned away trying to hide a forbidden half-smile of triumph.

"So what are you waiting for?"

"Wouldn't I be a fool to accept him now?"

"Julia!" Nora's expression and voice were exasperated. "Okay, I got it before, you had to make your own way, live a life that was entirely your own achievement. But now . . . you have done it, you have the success. You know yourself, trust yourself. Exactly what do you think he can take from you now?"

I narrowed my eyes and peered into the distance. I had no answer.

"Exactly! Nothing. So get over yourself. Let it happen."

I drove up a headland, parked and walked up the cliff path to the bluffs. I needed a vast view to absorb everything that was happening inside me. I don't know how long I stood there, braced against the wind, but when I returned to the car I was exhausted. I slept a few minutes before starting the engine and returning home.

57

"Simon," I said, taking his hand as he came in after work that evening and leading him to the sofa. "Do you know how much I appreciate what you have done for me, and for Maria?"

"It's nothing."

I looked at him properly for the first time in months.

"But I put you through so much."

"We both made mistakes."

"I just wanted to thank you."

"Why are you saying this? It sounds like goodbye."

"No, it's not goodbye. Not at all. I'm just sorting things out, making peace with the past."

I watched him as he looked down at his hands. He could feel something was different. He made a small sideways movement with his head, then looked up at me. "Well, then, you're welcome."

"I wanted to ask you something. Something that's been bothering me."

"Anything." But he looked worried, like he expected something bad.

"Did Lance . . ?" I didn't know how to continue. The wary expression on his face intensified.

"What? Did Lance what?"

"Did he ever, like, tell you about our sex life? God. I can't believe I'm asking you this. It was only a dream . . . but did he ever tell you . . ." I put my hand over my eyes. ". . . details?"

There was a still silence. I had expected an immediate disclaimer, a stretched joke, maybe, or an expostulation, but nothing. I uncovered my face and looked at him. He was pale as a ghost.

"He did?"

"Constantly. From the first time you did it. He told me what you liked, what you did to him, what you said, he even imitated the noises you made."

I sat down, my head in my hands. "Oh God."

"Like I said. We knew he was a bastard. That was partly what we loved."

"But it must have been awful. I'm so sorry." After a few moments, I looked up with improbable hope. "Do you think everything he said was true? He might have made some of it up." But no, the expression on Simon's face was anguished.

"No. We both know his boundaries. He was a cad, but he was totally transparent. He wasn't a liar."

"How did you stand it? Why did you keep coming back?"

"Because I loved you. I told you." To my surprise, a mischievous expression played on his lips. "And it was useful, too, some of it."

I blushed, thinking back to our first night together, how intuitive Simon had seemed. I had put it down to his generosity, his kindness, genetic similarity, but in the light of what he knew, it made more sense. I covered my face again. "Oh God. How embarrassing."

He came and knelt in front of me. "No, Julia. Beautiful. I wouldn't have changed a moment of those nights and days. Except the ending. I would have changed the ending. I'm sorry I left you. I should never have left you."

I reached out and cupped his face with my hand. "It's me who should apologise."

"Well, you could make it up to me." Behind the love in his eyes, the mischief was still there.

"How? How? Anything."

"Tell me I'm a good lover."

"You are a good lover. Great."

"Better than Lance?" There was uncertainty now, insecurity.

My mouth twitched. I wanted to laugh. This conversation would have been unthinkable a week ago, a day ago. Something in me had changed, and Simon, always my reflection, had changed with it. "Actually, yes, now that you come to mention it. You are better."

"And something else . . ."

"Yes?"

"I'm here."

I felt myself grin. It was the weirdest feeling.

He looked away, out the window. A smirk played on his mouth and he threw me a flirty glance. "So? Are we on again, then? You and me?"

I took my time answering, feeling through my body for any resistance or doubt. There was nothing.

"Well? Are we?"

"Yeah. We are."

~ ~ ~ ~ ~ ~ ~ ~ ~ ~ ~ ~ ~ ~ ~ ~

If you have enjoyed

Law of Attraction

Please email jennifer@jennifermanson.co.nz
to join my mailing list and receive information
about further publications, or see
www.jennifermanson.co.nz.

I welcome your feedback.

Please post your review on Facebook.
Search for "Jennifer Manson Author"

With my very great thanks,

Jennifer.